wild orchid

wild orchid

Beverley
Brenna

Red Deer PRESS

Published in Canada by Red Deer Press
195 Allstate Parkway, Markham, ON, L3R 4T8
www.reddeerpress.com

Published in the United States by Red Deer Press
311 Washington Street, Brighton, Massachusetts, 02135

Credits
Edited for the Press by Peter Carver
Copyedited by Carolyn Dearden
Cover and text design by Erin Woodward
Cover photo courtesy Veer. Small round-leaved orchid photo courtesy Arthur A. Stillborn.
Printed and bound in Canada by Friesens.

We acknowledge with thanks the Canada Council for the Arts, and the Ontario Arts Council for their support of our publishing program. We acknowledge the financial support of the Government of Canada through the Canada Book Fund (CBF) for our publishing activities.

Canada Council Conseil des Arts
for the Arts du Canada

ONTARIO ARTS COUNCIL
CONSEIL DES ARTS DE L'ONTARIO
50 YEARS OF ONTARIO GOVERNMENT SUPPORT OF THE ARTS
50 ANS DE SOUTIEN DU GOUVERNEMENT DE L'ONTARIO AUX ARTS

Library and Archives Canada Cataloguing in Publication
Brenna, Beverley A
Wild orchid / Beverley Brenna.
ISBN 0-88995-330-9
I. Title
PS8553.R382W54   2005   jC813'.54   C2005-904418-7

FSC
www.fsc.org
MIX
Paper from
responsible sources
FSC® C016245

*For my parents—thanks for the happy summers at
Waskesiu Lake*

A special thanks to my husband Dwayne and our sons, Wilson, Eric, and Connor, for your love and encouragement; thanks also to my mom—Myra Stilborn—and The Saskatchewan Arts Board, The Saskatchewan Writers Guild, St. Peter's Colony at Muenster, Shannon Friesen of Autism Treatment Services of Saskatchewan, Leona Theis, Brenda Baker, Guy Vanderhaeghe, Tony Attwood for your helpful academic texts, and Peter Carver—editor extraordinaire.

Saturday June 29
A Prologue

I can hear her banging around in the kitchen. The trouble is I'm not sure what she's thinking. Is she thinking about me? And if she is thinking about me, what will she do next?

I'm not behaving badly. In fact, I'm just sitting on my bed, and I have my door locked to prevent myself from being dragged out to the car. The problem is not the car. The problem is that I am not familiar with where we would be going. Also, I know that when people go away, it's possible that they don't come back.

Maybe she isn't mad. Maybe she's thinking about something else. . . . Maybe she saw a spider and is trying to disintegrate it with a broom. Or she could be tired and trying to decide whether to shatter the dishes instead of washing them.

I have calmed myself down from our recent discussion. I counted to a hundred, seven times, and found that to be very soothing. I know that when I'm angry, my IQ goes down sixty points, and I try not to let this happen. It is frightening to be stupid when I am not accustomed to it.

I was having a good day until we started to talk. I woke at exactly seven-thirty, right on schedule. I brushed my teeth and washed up, and then began to sort things into boxes. I am very good at sorting things. When she knocked on my door, I indicated that I did not want to be disturbed, but she came in anyway.

"What are you doing?" she said.

I thought it was fairly obvious what I was doing. I was sorting things into boxes. I told her so, and I could hear her voice stretch, trying to sound nice, but with that undertone of sharpness in it. A voice like a cupboard with scissors hidden inside.

"Taylor, remember, today is the day."

"Today is Saturday," I told her. "June 29."

"No," she said. "Come on. I've talked to you about this."

"You've talked to me about a lot of things," I said. "Too many, in my estimate."

"Don't start," she said. "We've already planned what's going to happen today."

"I have to get this place cleaned up," I said.

"Taylor Jane Simon, listen to me!" You could see the scissors in her voice, now.

"Snip, snap," I said.

This is when she got loud.

"Today is the day we are going to Waskesiu," she said, "whether you like it or not."

"I'm not going to Waskesiu," I said. "And you can't make me."

"Don't you want me to have a life!" she yelled. "Why can't you just do this one thing? You'd like it there if you gave it a chance."

"It isn't one thing," I said. "It might be one thing for you, but it's at least twenty things for me. Twenty new things. We're talking twenty to one, Mom."

She went out of my room and banged the door. It's not good to bang doors. It's hard on the hinges. It's good I locked the door, because now nobody will bang it again.

Examining My Argument

I've just counted them to make sure. It is at least twenty new things, and that's just the things that would happen before lunch. First there would be the highway, and we've never been on that highway before. Next, we would be entering Prince Albert National Park, and after that we would have to drive into the townsite on a narrow road, and then we'd go past the lake and pull up at the restaurant where her boyfriend, Danny Marsh, works. I've met Danny before, so he isn't really something new, but he talks in strings of words that add up to nine, and I think he's a bimbo. (Does *bimbo* work for males as well as females? I'll have to look it up.) Because of this, I like to pretend I don't know him; therefore, I can still count him as a new thing. We would have to go inside and then up some stairs, and I would have a new bedroom. I don't know what's inside the bedroom, but if I count a bed, a chest of drawers, a closet and a rug, that's four, and there's probably at least ten other foreign things in there that I don't know about. When I look out the window—because there's probably a window—there would be something outside that I've never seen before and likely more than one thing unless the window faces right into the lake and all I can see is water, which is highly unlikely because I know the bedroom isn't in a submarine.

So that's at least twenty unfamiliar things. I can see that I have been fair in the position I am taking: going to Waskesiu is not reasonable under the circumstances. The trouble with my mother is that she isn't very good at weighing decisions. She often just sees her side. It's a good thing she has me to help her with balance.

I put on some classical baroque music to listen to while I was sorting things, and I am still listening to it. Classical baroque music is very soothing. It is the only music I have found that does not filter thoughts out of my head while I am thinking them. For Christmas, Danny gave me a CD by a group called Barenaked Ladies. When I was listening to it, I forgot all sorts of things that I haven't remembered yet.

Now I can hear my mother loading up the car, and that suits me fine because she likes to be busy. I will just keep writing as long as I can because I think writing is a good escape. Plus, it lets you examine events from a safe distance. Wasn't it Aristotle who said, "The pen is mightier than the sword?" He meant that you could write instead of fight. That is what I am doing now, since I am done my sorting. I wonder why my mother is loading up the car when we aren't going anywhere. She is often illogical. I imagine she was just born that way.

My Inspiration for Keeping a Journal

I have my English teacher to thank for the idea of keeping this journal. My ex-English teacher, I mean. Thinking about being done high school is a ten on the scale of scary thoughts, and I try not to dwell on it, but when Mrs. Thomson was giving me an oral exam, I started unloading some of my grief about the future. My oral exam was on *The Catcher in the Rye* by J.D. Salinger. I had to do an oral exam because, on the written exam, the teacher asked us to think about the ending and draw our own conclusions. I drew stuff all over the page, and she said that wasn't what she had intended. She said that she had meant for us to write an essay to answer what might happen next. Usually I am very good at writing essays, and I was disappointed not to have gotten to write this one. I would rather write an essay than do any other kind of writing. I would even rather write an essay than talk.

Anyhow, when we were talking about the novel, I said that Holden and I are exactly alike except for the following:

1. He is sixteen or seventeen, and I am eighteen and a half.
2. He has a red hunting cap.
3. He has had a relationship with a member of the opposite sex and I have not, although this is one of my aspirations.

She asked me in what ways I think we're alike, and I said that most of the time, like Holden, I'm mad and disgusted with people, which is true. I also said that he wasn't looking forward to much and that I'm the same way. She advised me to keep a journal and said that sometimes it feels good to let off steam in print. I said I didn't know what that meant, and she said it meant that sometimes writing stuff down makes you feel better.

Later, I thought of another difference between Holden and me: Holden was allowed to swear in print, while I have this stupid lock my teachers put on the laptop so that certain words won't get through—they just come up blank if you try to type them. When you're trying to swear, nothing is more immature than a blank, so I've decided to stick in the symbol !!&%$%@@@ to represent a swear word. Not perfect, but it's the best I can do.

How I Ended Up Going to Waskesiu After All

Mom wrote me a note explaining why we have to go to Waskesiu and pushed it under my door. She said that she had signed a contract to work in Danny's restaurant for the summer and that this contract is legal and binding. I asked if there were any loopholes in the contract and could I see it and she said no to both questions. Even though I can count at least eighty-seven reasons why I do not want to go to Waskesiu, when a person is faced with a legal contract, you have to give in.

I had a good idea, though. I asked if we could make up a contract saying that we are coming home for sure at the end of the summer, and she agreed to that. I wrote up the contract and we both signed it, and so at least I have some assurance of regularity once the summer is over. This is somewhat reassuring, even though I will be in the future by then and I have no idea what I will be doing. But I don't want to think about scary thoughts, especially if they are tens.

The drive to Waskesiu sucked. I don't like sitting still, and I especially don't like sitting still while perceiving that things around me are moving. I know that really I am moving, while everything else outside the car is stationary, but it feels like the other way around. In the car I sat with my pillow behind my neck and my window blind down. I don't like bright sunlight and today turned into a very bright day. That's one reason I don't like the color yellow—it reminds me too much of sunlight. Also, it makes me sneeze.

"How much longer?" I asked when we reached Duck Lake.

"We're about halfway," said Mom.

"About halfway or exactly halfway?" I said.

"Get the map and figure it out for yourself," she said, so I did. Just as I had thought: We were not exactly halfway, but considerably less, which was not very comforting. A town called MacDowell was halfway, and I kept quiet until we got there.

"I see that Waskesiu is still in Saskatchewan," I said when I was speaking again. "And it's even still in Canada. That's good. So we can use the same money."

"Of course we'll use the same money," Mom said. "Don't make more of this than you need to!"

I wasn't sure what she meant by that, but it sounded like a fight starting and I decided to keep quiet again.

We stopped in Prince Albert for gas, and I walked around the car seven times.

"You're not going to start that counting thing again, are you?" Mom asked when I got back into the car. Sometimes, she really makes me mad. I wish she'd just lay off and take a pill or something. No, forget that. I don't really mean it. I took medication for a while, when I was eight, just after my father left. They thought I was having some sort of reaction to him going—posttraumatic stress, they called it. I was having a lot of meltdowns, and at school, I insisted on sitting inside a cardboard box that was left after a new computer had arrived.

Anyway, the medication made me feel like !!&%&%@@@ and didn't help my meltdowns or my preference for being in the box. After a few months, they cancelled my prescription.

I think Dad left because of my problems. For sure they didn't suddenly appear once he was gone—they just changed in degree with the added stress. I think him leaving really sucked. Being a good parent is helping your kids when they have problems, not disappearing.

"Start that counting thing again?" I said to Mom, pretending not to know what she was talking about. Shauna taught me that one way to carry on a conversation with someone is to repeat part of the sentence they say to you, and I find that sometimes I can use it to my advantage. Teacher associates are good for particular learning, such as discovering the dynamics of conversations. They really inhibit your love life, though, because boys don't want to hit on a girl who is sitting with a teacher associate.

"You know what I am talking about," Mom said.

"You know what I am talking about," I repeated. "Seven words."

"Don't you dare start," she said.

I have this feeling that the number seven is lucky, and if I do things seven times, I feel safe. Like, I'll take seven little sips from my glass instead of one big one, or bounce a ball seven times. Going around the car seven times was a necessary diversion for my anxious feelings. The fact that her words came out in sevens was just a lucky event.

"Maybe it was an accident," I said.

Mom squeezed her eyebrows together so that there was an H in the middle of her forehead. This is a signal she has. It means she is worried and cross.

"Drink your water," she said. "It'll help you relax." Then she got back in the car. I got in beside her.

"I am relaxed," I said.

"*Someone's* starting to talk back," she said.

"*Someone's* not my name," I answered. Then I said, "!!&%$%@@@," but quietly, under my breath, so she wouldn't freak out. Even though I am officially an adult and should be able to say what I like, my mother takes great exception to swear words.

What made me mad in this situation is that I have this thing about names. It seems to me that a name really defines the person or thing it describes. Names are important. If I get called by something other than my actual name, such as *someone*, I start feeling light-headed and anonymous. I've told my mother not to do it, but sometimes she forgets.

"Try to be good to yourself," she went on. "And to me. Do what you need to do. Remember that this summer is important to me. I really want it to work out in Waskesiu. I'll be pretty busy, so I'm counting on you to take care of yourself. Remember the social story we made about being independent?"

"Everyone gets into new situations sometimes," I quoted. "Sometimes, new situations can be scary. When I'm in new situations, I'll try to remember the things that help me feel good. I can drink water from my water bottle. I can make lists of what I need to do. I can take a body break!" I didn't mean to, but I raised my voice into the red zone and kept it there. "I know all that, Mom! I can take care of myself!"

"Lower your voice. Just remember to think positive."

I picked up my water bottle to make her stop talking, but I didn't drink much. Just enough to make her quit reminding me. I did feel more relaxed afterward. Chewing gum has the same effect, but I had all of mine packed.

"Got any gum?" I asked.

Mom fished out a package of Trident and I took out a piece.

"Offer me some," she said.

"Offer you some?"

"It's nice to offer me some. I'm driving and shouldn't be fiddling around opening gum wrappers, so it would be nice if you offered."

"Do you want a piece?" I asked.

"No thanks, but maybe in a little while. You can keep the package." It's so like my mother to tell me one thing and then, in the next breath, change the rules. Why wouldn't she want a piece of gum when she had just told me to ask her? She calls it being *spontaneous*. She says that you have to learn the scripts for social situations and then expect that the responses might be different than what you would predict. And people think I'm weird!

By the time we pulled up to the entrance gate, I had to go to the bathroom. I ran into the little building Mom called an outhouse, but I ran right out again. The outhouse was gross. I couldn't believe it was a bathroom. Mom motioned me back in, and since I really had to go, I took her advice, but who would have thought that a substitute for a toilet was a hole in the ground with a wooden seat on top of it? What a stench! I hoped the bathrooms where we'd be staying wouldn't be like this. I almost didn't use it, but the alternative would have been worse, so I held my breath and did my business. When I came out, I couldn't get the tap on the fake sink to work, and I started to get ticked off at the thought of not washing my hands. Then Mom came over and showed me what to press, and I finished the job. Mom paid our entrance fee to the national park. Then we drove farther along the highway to the townsite.

"We're so lucky we get to stay right beside the lake," Mom said. "I bet you can't wait to see what your room will look like."

"Does it have an outhouse?" I asked, starting to hyperventilate, and she shoved my water bottle at me again.

"Don't be silly. Of course not. Take a drink. First we'll unpack. Then we'll go have a walk on the beach. One thing at a time, Taylor; take one thing at a time."

"First unpack, then the beach," I repeated, relieved that there'd be a regular bathroom. "Do you think there will be any boys my age on the beach?" I asked.

Mom nodded. "Probably," she said.

"Good," I said. "Because one of my goals this summer is to have a boyfriend. I think it's really about time."

"Uh-huh," said Mom. "I'm sure you will meet lots of new people in Waskesiu."

"I don't really care about new people," I said. "Because new people, if you are using that term correctly, would refer to babies. I would prefer a boyfriend my own age."

Mom laughed when I said that, and I told her to stop laughing and watch the road. Sometimes, she gets a bit hysterical and her attention wanders. It could be PMS. Or maybe menopause. Either one can make you unsteady.

The Foreign Bedroom

We pulled up beside a building that had *Pizza Penny's* on a sign above the window. Boy, that really was funny—seeing Mom's name on the place—funny peculiar, not funny ha-ha.

"I don't like Danny, and I don't want to live here," I said.

"What's there not to like?" said Mom. "He's a good guy, and he's giving us this great place to stay for a holiday."

"He always talks in odd numbers," I said. "Usually in nines."

"Don't be silly. He does not."

"He does. You count him sometime, you'll see. And his hair is juicy."

"Never mind. Just put your best foot forward."

This is a perplexing request. As far as I can tell, my feet are identical under any circumstances requiring evaluation.

We got out of the car, and I pulled my suitcase out of the back seat. Carrying something heavy made me feel less like freaking out. I dropped my face to the rough, zippered top of the suitcase and sniffed. It smelled like Hammy. My gerbil died this year, and the old cage is stored in the cubby under the stairs, where the suitcase usually sits.

"What are you doing?" Mom asked sharply.

"My suitcase smells like Hammy," I said.

"Don't start," warned Mom.

"Hammy lived to be four years old. That was fairly old for a gerbil. Before Hammy, I had Charlotte, and before her, I had June, and before her, I had Walnut, and he was the first gerbil I ever had."

"What kind of a day is it, Taylor? Look at the sky—is it clear or cloudy?"

I heard Mom, but I had to finish what I was saying about gerbils or things would get out of control.

"Gerbils are rodents. They can also be described as small mammals. They are nocturnal, and, although they make good pets, they do make noise in their cages at night. They drum with their feet against the metal floor. This is their best way of communicating."

"Taylor! Quit already!"

"What!"

"Don't you dare get onto this subject now! Quit worrying! Everything will be fine. You'll like it here. Stand up tall. First unpack, then the beach." She gave me a little rub on the back and then opened the door of the restaurant.

I stuck some fresh gum in my mouth and followed her in. The smell of pizza was everywhere. Strong odors make me dizzy, and it was all I could do to walk after Mom down the hall and into the back room, where we found Danny in an office, sitting at a desk. He had his feet up on the desk. That's not very hygienic, I wanted to tell him, but I kept quiet.

"Hey, I've been waiting for you!" he said, hugging my mother. "Like the sign?"

I looked at her to see if she had noticed the nine words, but she was busy examining the certificates on his wall. Danny reached out to take my suitcase, but I climbed on top of it. No way he was going to touch my things.

"Taylor, get off your suitcase!" yelled Mom. Now she was the one talking in the red zone.

"I can carry it," I said. I wasn't being polite. I just didn't want him touching my things. Danny rubbed his hands through his oily hair, and then he led us through the kitchen and up some stairs into a hallway with three rooms: two bedrooms and a bathroom at the end of the hall.

"Go ahead, Taylor. Unpack, get comfortable. Unwind a bit," he said to me, opening the door to one of the bedrooms.

Unwind. That's an odd word. It reminds me of the spring in my clock. But a person's not a spring. How could I unwind?

Watching Danny open the door was disgusting. Great, I thought, he's got !!&%$%@@@ hair juice on the doorknob. I pushed the door all the way open with my foot. Then he picked up my mother and carried her through the doorway of the second bedroom, shutting the door behind them. He sort of dragged her, rather than carried her, because he's not a big man—not any bigger than my mom. I could hear them laughing, though, so I knew she didn't mind.

I pushed my suitcase toward the bed, turned around and shut the door. And then I looked at the walls. They were yellow. I said some bad words and then started yelling for Mom. In a minute she came running in.

"What's wrong? What's the matter?" she asked, Danny close behind her.

I couldn't speak for a minute. In my head all I could think of were swears. Then I sneezed.

"It's kind of strange, getting used to a new place," she said, sitting down on the bed and pulling me down beside her.

"!!&%$%@@@," I blurted, bouncing a little on the mattress.

"Take some deep breaths. Try not to use that bad language, Taylor. Remember we've talked about this. Try to think of the words to tell me what's bothering you. Is it because you had to sit so long in the car?"

"No, it's not that!" I yelled. "Look at the walls. They're !!&%$%@@@ yellow!" I screamed, way beyond the volume of even the red zone. By this time I was really bouncing.

"Taylor. Stop swearing! Take some more deep breaths. Okay, you're right—they are yellow," she said, looking up at Danny. "And I know you hate yellow. And we'll figure out a way to solve this for you. . . ."

"I have all my stuff in the other room," he said, and there was a pause while I just sat and bounced.

"And the bed in the other room is bigger. . . ."

I bounced even harder.

"We could move the bed," said Mom. "It wouldn't be such a big deal, would it, to move your stuff in here? You and I could do it right now, before anyone gets really upset, and while we're moving the bed, Taylor could go and have a walk on the beach."

"I don't want to walk on the !!&%$%@@@ beach," I said. "Remember, you said we were going to !!&%$%@@@ unpack first and then have a !!&%$%@@@ walk on the beach! It was unpack, then walk!"

"Stop swearing this minute!" said Mom. She grabbed my hands and pressed hard against the palms. "It would just be a little change of plans. First the walk and then the unpacking. Okay, Danny?"

"Sure, fine. It's no big problem. We can manage," he said, rubbing his fingers through his hair again. It gives me the creeps to watch him do that. I know that tonight when I'm trying to sleep, my mind will replay pictures of him rubbing his hair and then touching things in the room that I will be in. I hope that when I find a boyfriend, he will not have juicy hair.

I took some little steps around the room, and Mom gave me money to keep in my purse in case I needed anything. Then I went and had my walk while they moved Danny's things, and I tried not to imagine him touching anything in the room. When I came back, my suitcase was by my bed and the door to the yellow room was shut. I just knew that Danny had touched my suitcase. I swallowed hard and looked around. The walls were green. I had been hoping hard that they would be blue, but green wasn't too bad. I figured I could handle green.

Clocks and Why They Are Necessary

First I unpacked a pair of shorts that I never wear and rubbed my suitcase with them to clean it. Then I unpacked my alarm clock. I love my alarm clock. It has an entirely predictable face. It's an old-fashioned design that stands on four little legs. The case is a nice sky blue and the clock face is white. I've had it ever since I was a little kid. There's a toggle on the back that you have to crank every night. It works on the principle of springs that unwind according to schedule if they are tightened in the opposite direction. Mom occasionally talks about getting me a new one because she thinks it looks old and chipped, but I think that the minor alterations in color are not a problem.

When I went to see Dad last Christmas, I forgot to take my clock. Because I'd forgotten it, I had to go out to the kitchen and look at the big clock above the table. This meant that at night, when I got into bed, I had to get out again when I wanted to check the time. Knowing the exact time is important when you're calculating how much sleep you're going to get, and in this case, to be precise, I also had to subtract the time it took to walk back from the kitchen from the actual time that I'd read on the clock. I like math, but doing equations like this isn't exactly relaxing.

When you're out of the house, it's easy to check the time. Clocks, I have noticed, are everywhere. Inside, though, it's a different matter. Dad offered to buy me a watch, but I don't get along very well with watches. They always lose or gain time, I'm not sure why, and there's nothing worse than having a timepiece that isn't correct. I've had watches before, and mostly I just took them apart and made mobiles out of them. That's one way to make your parents freak out—casually letting them see a mobile hanging in your room that's made out of watch guts. Anyway, not having the clock was probably the beginning of the end of my visit to Dad's.

Today, after I put the alarm clock beside my bed, I took out my dictionary and looked up *bimbo*. It wouldn't work for Danny after all because it refers to women. Why are there words that refer to women and not to men when they need virtually the same definition, such as, "person who is stupid"? Once again, old *Oxford English* is letting me down.

Next, I organized my clothes in the drawers. Some of the drawers still had Danny's things in them, but two empty ones were big enough to hold all my things. I put my sandals in the drawer with my underwear because I only wear running shoes, not sandals. I hung my dresses in the closet—I brought a jean dress that I really like and two others that I don't like—and then I sat down on the bed with my laptop on my knees. After a minute, I pulled up a chair and set the laptop on it. I remember hearing a story about someone who got their private parts burnt from using a laptop on their lap for too long. I wonder why they're called laptops if they're not supposed to sit on your lap?

All of this unpacking took me seventeen minutes. I estimated that it would take between fifteen and twenty minutes, and so when I calculated seventeen minutes, I wasn't surprised. That's the thing about clocks. They never surprise you. They are completely reasonable.

When I reread what I've just written, there are a few things I remember about today that I've forgotten to put down. Like when I walked on the beach, I went back and forth seven times. Good thing Mom wasn't there to watch as this would have made her mad. I used to think that Mom would feel the same way about things as I did. This was before I learned that people can have different perspectives on something. One person can look out the window and see their grandmother getting out of a car. When the doorbell rings, that person will know who is at the door. Another person in the kitchen who didn't see the car will not know who is at the door. That person needs to be told. This is why words are very important. They are the bridges between people's thoughts. I have tried to explain to my mother that when you need to do something seven times to feel relaxed, it's just better to do it and enjoy the outcome. So far she does not agree with me.

Most people would agree with my mother, which makes me a minority. However, this does not mean that I am wrong. In fact, I would argue that I am correct. It is better to do the thing that makes you relaxed as long as it's not hurting anyone else. At least, that's my experience. What confuses me most is how I can take one perspective on something and then find out that others think differently. It's like walking into a room where everything is blue and saying, "So, everything is blue in here," and having everybody look at you funny and say, "There isn't any blue in here. What's wrong with you, you geek!"

This file is to share my thoughts and feelings, like my English teacher said, but more importantly, it's to help me sort things out. Preferably before I do something dumb. However, I know that being dumb is human. So I don't mind being dumb. With the following qualifiers:

1. I don't want to look dumb around my mother's boyfriend because he is dumb and that would make two of us.

2. I don't want to look dumb around my mother because she'll say, "I told you so."

3. I don't want to look dumb around boys.

I wonder if I have chosen the right title for this section. It did start to be about clocks, but then it changed to another topic—the purpose of this journal. This essay could be construed as rambling. However, because I have adopted a fairly informal style, I think this is okay. Since two thirds of the essay is about clocks, I am justified in the title, and so I will keep it.

Boys

There is one other thing I am thinking about tonight besides trying to adjust to this new place, and that's boys. I'm hoping that this summer I'll meet a boy and that this boy will find something about me to like. People have told me that I am quite a good-looking girl. I have long, black hair and rosy cheeks. I also have long, dark eyelashes—and this is lucky because I don't need mascara—and blue eyes. Blue eyes and dark hair is a nice combination, my mother says. She just has brown hair and blue eyes, and that's more common. Looking common hasn't seemed to hold her back, though. Lots of men like her.

I have noticed that she always picks the same type of man to date. I wonder why she doesn't just pick the same man rather than the same type of man. I mean, it would be much more reasonable if she just dated the same person. Then she would know him, and there wouldn't have to be more than one first date. The first date is the scariest, in my opinion, because there is so much about the other person that you don't know. I always find Mom's first dates very disconcerting. Feeling this way makes me nervous about how I will manage my own first date, if I ever have one. And I hope I do, even if it makes me exhausted because that is part of growing up.

Mom's boyfriends always have dark hair and big lips, and wear golf shirts and polyester pants. They usually wear dark socks and loafers. They are always about her height, or a few centimeters taller, and smell like aftershave. They all have bad habits. Some of them belch really loudly. Some of them scratch places where you're not supposed to scratch. One of them smoked. That's something I cannot put up with, a person who smokes. It is so disgusting for your lungs, let alone the other people around you. As if all the burping and scratching and smoking isn't enough, these boyfriends have voices that sound like they come through their noses, and they laugh a lot for no reason. I'm not too good about looking at faces, but if I was, I bet their faces would all look the same   fish faces to match their lips.

All of the boys I know are from my high school, and none of them wear golf shirts. Some of them talk to me, but none of them are boyfriend material because they think of me as someone who has special needs. When I'm eating lunch, sometimes boys sit at my table, but only if there are other girls there. Not once has a boy ever come to eat lunch just with me. Shauna, the teacher associate who worked with me, used to pick out a cute guy every now and then and ask me what I thought of him, but I'm not really that discerning. Jeans are nice. If they're wearing jeans, I think they look good.

Mom says that Danny is a nine, and I should give him a chance. I'm not sure what she means by this, but maybe she's noticed that he really does say nine words at a time. Maybe anything under ten is economical and considered a positive characteristic. She also says I should be grateful for the opportunity to get away for the summer. She has booked time off her other job and says she has it coming. She thinks about this as a nice little intermission from secretary work, and then she'll go back to her same old job after the summer is done. For me, it's something new, to be followed by the future, which, so far, is just a black hole sucking me inward. I'm starting to feel sick to my stomach thinking about it.

Now I'm wondering about what I'm going to do next because we haven't really planned it out yet. It was to be unpacking and then walking; it ended up being walking and then unpacking. I am disappointed that I didn't notice any boys on the beach when I was down there. How am I going to get a boyfriend if I can't even see a boy?

Now what? If this is "unwinding," then I guess I'm not very good at it. I am sitting on the bed bouncing between each word that I write. "What? What? What? What? What? What? What?" Oops, that was seven times. "What?" There, that makes it eight, and there's nothing Mom would say about !!&%$%@@@ eight!

My Thoughts on Beaches and Parties

After I wrote the last essay, I started feeling really stressed so I put on my jean dress. Then I called Mom until she came and made a list on paper of the things I could do and told me when I should be back for supper. Then I went downstairs with Mom and Danny for lunch, and we had pizza.

"So, Taylor, what are your plans for the future?" Danny asked in his typical, nine-word fashion.

"I find it disconcerting to be asked about plans I haven't got," I said. "Maybe I'll start a gerbil ranch."

"Taylor," said Mom. She had the H in wrinkles on her forehead.

"Well, I might," I said and took seven sips of water. The future is not a subject to think about when I am eating.

"What do you think of my pizza? Pretty good?" asked Danny. Nine again. I didn't answer. "Do you always order just cheese? Or other kinds?" he persisted.

"Cheese is my favorite," I said. It makes me feel cross when people ask my opinion of things because I have to stop and think for a minute about perspectives. They do not know what I am thinking unless I tell them. This makes life complicated. It would be easier if everybody just felt the same way, and then you wouldn't need to talk about it.

I watched Danny while he was eating. His mouth was a bit like the hole in a squid's face. He divided up his pizza and ate the crust first and then used a knife and fork to eat the rest. That was weird. His hair is so slimy that maybe he uses olive oil on it. I bet he does—he probably buys it in bulk. I kept trying to think of his movie twin, and then, just when I was finishing my chocolate milk, it came to me. Danny de Vito! I saw him recently in the DVD of *Throw Momma from the Train.*

Throw Penny from the Pier. I hoped that wasn't what he was planning, to do away with my mom so he'd get the inheritance. Of course, he wasn't reckoning on my being around to claim it. . . . Maybe he was poisoning my pizza! I knew this wasn't true, but somehow it just seemed to fit. Something about Danny made me want to !!&%$%@@@ puke.

After lunch, I went out for a walk. Danny gave me a map of the town so I wouldn't get lost. I looked at it carefully when I got out into the sun, thinking maybe he had given me the map so that I *would* get lost. Lost so that when the poisoning took effect nobody could help me. I could see his oily fingerprints on the map. At least the police would have a way to identify the killer.

I went back to the beach, and because it was a warm day, I took off my running shoes and tried walking in the water. I have seen people doing this in movies. The water was cold and the sand felt invasive against my feet, so I brushed myself off and put on my shoes. Families with kids were playing in the sand, and some people were swimming. I didn't look at anyone, just minded my own business and walked past. When I got to the end of the beach, there was the playground and one swing was free, so I sat on it and spun for a while. That felt really good.

There's a couple of autism websites I've gone on, and I remember a questionnaire I saw on one of them. The first question was:

When you go to the beach, do you want to

a. Lay down your towel and stretch out in the sun?

b. Kick off your sandals and run into the waves?

c. Get off the beach as soon as possible?

Of course I picked *c*. I got a total of eighty-five points out of a hundred for my answers to the questions, and at the end of the quiz, everyone with over seventy-five points gets a message that says, "Congratulations, you're definitely autistic!" I got the message.

I have a particular form of autism called Asperger's Syndrome. When I was ten, the doctor told my mother the diagnosis, and when I was eleven, she told me. "I think you're old enough to know," she said. At first, I thought she was saying, "Ass Burgers." Later, when she asked if I had told anyone at school, I said, "Of course not." I mean, who would go around telling people they had *Ass Burgers*.

When I was in grade five, Mom told the people at my school about my diagnosis, and I started getting more help. A teacher associate named Janet worked with me. The government paid for it, and, later, they paid for Shauna when Janet went off to have a baby. When I started doing really well at some things, like writing and math, my dad let me come to Cody, Wyoming, to visit him. I don't think that's right, to wait until your kids do well and then invite them to visit. I think you should be a parent whether the kids do well or not.

One of the other questions on the quiz read:

When you go to a party, do you

a. Say hi to the person opening the door and give them a little gift you've purchased for the house.

b. Go to the buffet table and help yourself to a snack.

c. Search around the house until you find an empty room and then sit in it.

I picked *c,* and earned more points. My preference for empty rooms could be why I've never really enjoyed parties. The kind of parties I hate the most are birthday parties, although I have heard of something called beach parties, and I assume that they are the worst. My own birthday parties were disasters, but I don't want to get into that now. Nobody ever invites me to parties anymore, and on the one hand, that's a good thing because I would probably go around looking for an empty room, but on the other hand, that's a bad thing because parties are a good place to meet eligible boys—that is, boys who are looking for girl friends.

How I Almost Met a Boy

While I was swinging at the playground, I started counting things, and then I noticed that I was making sure to find seven of whatever it was I was counting, and it was taking a long time. Imagine trying to find seven kids with red buckets on a crowded beach! So I said to myself, *That's enough of that,* and got up and went back down the beach toward a path through some evergreens. Just before I reached the trees, I passed a bunch of people playing beach volleyball, and one of the boys called out to me. I didn't answer, but just walked past, and then I heard someone whistle. Could the boy have been whistling at me?

I should have stopped because I'll never get a boyfriend if I don't talk to any boys, but I just couldn't make myself. I was hot and all I wanted to do was get off the beach, just like on the questionnaire.

When I was walking down the path, I looked around at the trees and realized I was in a small forest, although it was still part of the townsite. I recently saw a TV rerun of the first Indiana Jones' movie, *Raiders of the Lost Ark*, and, although this area does not look like a jungle, I wondered if there might be snakes. I do not like snakes. I saw a building up ahead, and I was happy to go into it. When I got inside, I looked on the map and discovered it was called a nature center. The temperature inside was about twenty-two degrees, and I felt like I was walking into a safe place with dim lights in contrast to the bright day. The air smelled like wood—a nice smell, not too strong—and I took a big breath.

"You sound like you've had a hard go of it." A man was sitting at a table, and on the table was an aquarium full of plants.

I didn't feel like answering because I wasn't sure whether I should agree with him or not, so I walked around the room and looked at the displays. There was only one other person there, a girl who was taking books out of a cardboard box and putting them on a shelf. She had blonde hair in braids and reminded me of Judy Garland from *The Wizard of Oz*, and I stood and stared at her for a moment until I remembered that staring isn't polite. When I got back to the part of the room near the man, I took a closer look at what he was doing. He had some small plants in plastic bags, and he was transplanting them into the aquarium.

"Do you know any of the names of these?" he asked, not looking up. I appreciated the fact that he didn't look at me—it made having a conversation much more comfortable.

"No," I said, going over and looking at the plants.

"This one's a sundew. See the tiny hairs on the leaves—it's like a Venus's-flytrap, and it catches insects."

"How does it do that?" I asked.

"These hairs sweat out a sticky fluid that traps small bugs that land on them," he answered, gently prying open one of the leaves. "This one's a spatulate-leaved sundew because the leaves are spoon shaped. All the plants I have here are bog varieties." I counted his specimens. There were seven.

"Bog varieties?" I repeated.

"Yeah. This one here is a pitcher plant." He touched the large flower head of a curious, nodding, dark red bloom with a thick stem and pitcher-shaped leaves. "The leaves are hollow and hold water, which drowns insects."

I sniffed. I could smell what must be the odor of the bog. The pitcher plant and the sundew must be very sensitive plants. I read somewhere that some plants have a sense of touch, kind of like people do. When they feel a bug landing on them, they suck the insect into their trap. Some plants are more touch sensitive than others, I guess, just like people.

"Got these all on the Bog Trail. Are you familiar with it?" the guy asked.

"No," I said, looking closely at the name tag he was wearing. It said his name was Paul.

"A group is going from here tomorrow at ten. Join us if you like."

"There aren't any snakes on the Bog Trail, are there?" I asked.

"Likely not," said Paul. "We don't have any poisonous snakes in the park. Just the occasional garter snake or two."

I nodded because sometimes that's just as good as answering in words. Garter snakes wouldn't be that bad, although I would rather swim, eat crunchy foods or go back to that yellow bedroom than see one of them.

"We have a film starting in five minutes, if you have the time to stay," he went on. I looked around and saw that other people had entered the nature center. They must have known about the film because they made their way to a door at the back of the room. Must be the theater, I thought, following them. I like theaters. They are cool and quiet, except for the movie at the front which is nothing that can hurt you because it's just on a screen. Even so, sometimes a theater would be better without the movie. I generally prefer to watch movies at home on DVD. This time, though, the movie in the theater was good.

It was about orchids. I had heard of them, of course, but had no idea that there were so many wild ones that grow in Canada. There are a few to look for here: the yellow lady's slipper, the white lady's slipper—but it's supposed to be extinct now in Saskatchewan—the sparrow's egg lady's slipper, which looks a lot like the white one, and a pink one called Venus's slipper, which is also very rare. There are apparently twenty-five different kinds of orchids in Saskatchewan, twenty-six if the white lady's slipper wasn't extinct. While I watched the film, I had an idea. I could look for these orchids while I was living in Waskesiu. It would give me a hobby. Because this is a national park, you're not allowed to pick any of the flowers, so I decided I wouldn't pick any.

Orchids are the most bizarre flowers I've ever heard of. They can be shaped like buckets, slippers, helmets, even flying ducks. Some mimic female wasps or bees so that males try to mate with the flowers, and when they do this, they pollinate them. There is a very strange word for this process, and it's *pseudocopulation.* The word flashed across the screen as they showed a film sequence of this happening, and good thing it did, or I would never have remembered it, let alone known how to spell it. When I see something, though, like a word spelled out, I can review it on the inside of my eyelids.

The slipper orchids got their name because of the bottom petal. The top two petals are elliptical, but the bottom one is curled up into the shape of a moccasin. I am interested in these species, and I hope to find out more about them. The one I'd like to see most is the white lady's slipper because it's extinct here, but I probably never will. The one I'd like to see second most is the Venus's slipper. My third choice would be the sparrow's egg.

The most interesting thing I discovered about orchids is that to thrive, they require a balance of heredity and environment. The seed must fall on a special kind of fungus that allows it to germinate. Orchids have a reputation for being difficult to grow—they are unusually discerning plants that need a home devoted to their unique needs.

Funny, though, that what I remember most about today is not the orchids. It's the man who was replanting the bog specimens. He was wearing khaki pants and a shirt with a crest over one pocket, and a brown Tilley hat. He had longish brown hair that crept out from under the hat, and a short brown beard. He had a soft voice that was not high or low, just somewhere in the middle, and brown boots. His hands were tanned, but you could see where the shirt pulled back that his arms were lighter. He reminds me of Indiana Jones, although I really didn't get a good look at his face.

Now it's time for bed. I hope I will sleep. I am afraid I will not sleep, but maybe sleep will come as a surprise. I will try very hard not to replay the pictures in my mind of Danny rubbing his hair and then touching my suitcase, but I know they are lying in wait on the inside of my eyelids. I am also worrying about what I should have done when the boy whistled at me.

I have never been whistled at before. It was an interesting experience. Should I have whistled back?

Sunday June 30
Churches and Forests

Because today is Sunday, I expected I would go to church, but I forgot that I am too far from my church in Saskatoon. I can't go to church here in Waskesiu for the simple fact that there isn't a church. I am unhappy about this because I'm used to going to church every Sunday, and I do not like a change in routine.

I am also glad because I do not like church. It is a time where there is a lot of sitting and very little fun. Until I turned twelve, Mom dropped me off at Sunday school. Then, after that, she said I was old enough to go to church with the adults. She says that church is another place I will meet people and make friends. So far I have not made any, but she says this doesn't matter and that church is a still a good place for me to go.

I have asked her numerous times why she does not go to church. She simply says that it's not her bag—this is another way of saying it's not something she likes to do—and that she has other ways to make friends. I have asked her why I can't use these other ways, but she just laughs and says that everybody's different and that as long as I am under her roof, I will be a church-going person. I know that when I am at church she often goes over to a boyfriend's house, and maybe this has to do with one of the ways she makes friends and I do not. One of her boyfriends lived right across the street from the church. She used to say this was very convenient. He had a big mole on his left ear that looked like an earring. It wasn't an earring, though; it was a mole.

One time I asked my mother about techniques for finding a boyfriend, and she just laughed. She said, "All in good time." This is not a rational statement because time has no affect: it cannot be either good or bad. It just exists. I think that my mother does not want me to have a boyfriend because this will mean that I am growing up, and she doesn't want me to cross over the line and be an adult. Possibly, she likes being the only adult in the house. I have news for her: you cannot stop a person from growing up. Some lines have to be crossed.

This morning when we had breakfast, I asked her about Danny. I asked her why she said he was a nine, and did it have to do with the nine words.

"What nine words?" she asked.

"The nine words he always says strung together," I answered.

"Don't be silly," she said. "Nine is his rating out of ten. A perfect guy would be a ten. Someone like Matt Damon would be a ten."

"Matt Damon smokes in every movie I've seen him in," I said. "He couldn't be a ten."

"Lighten up," she said. "Lots of people smoke, but they're still good people."

"I don't think so," I said. "Smoking is bad, right?"

"Well, right," she said.

"So people who smoke are bad. And I will never smoke."

"Well, that's one good thing," she said. Then Danny came and sat down, and I couldn't think of anything more to say, except to ask him what kind of salad oil he uses on his hair.

"Italian," he said briefly, breaking his usual tradition, but I think he was kidding.

The one thing about church I do like is the quiet and how it's okay to be quiet. It is much easier to breathe when it is quiet. The church I go to has a cathedral ceiling and stained glass windows along one side. I generally face the side without the windows, sitting forward, but turning my head to avoid the sunlight. It smells nice in church, too, a quiet, soft, powdery smell that may come from the people, but which could also be part of the building itself.

Today, I went to the nature center at ten for the Bog Trail walk, and when we started along the path into the woods, it felt to me like I was in church. Forests and churches are similar, except that in the forest you can't sit still because mosquitoes want to bite you. I used spray on any parts of my skin that were showing, and I think the other people did, too. Mosquitoes don't usually like me very much. This might be because I don't eat bananas. I read that mosquitoes are attracted to people who have eaten bananas. I don't eat bananas because they are yellow, and they make my mouth itch, as if it would want to sneeze if it were my nose.

There are seven ways that forests and churches are alike:

1. They both have quiet sounds in them that do not demand much of you.

2. They have a lot of air in them, but it doesn't enter as wind.
3. People talk in softer voices inside forests as well as churches.
4. You feel as though you're in the shade.
5. Both the walls and the trees stretch up high on either side of you.
6. There is a minty smell.
7. Both *forest* and *church* have six letters.

There were twelve of us in the group. Paul, the guy I met yesterday, was our leader. I wanted to walk at the front of the line because that is the place I am the most comfortable. I was the first one to find a sundew, and I pointed out pitcher plants that the others probably would not have seen without me as these plants were hidden behind tall marsh grass. I know that Danny's last name is Marsh, and I wish it wasn't. I will try to push him out of my mind when I see the marsh plants, or it will be like I am seeing him everywhere. He would make the kind of plant that bugs would stick to.

Paul said that I was a good detective to see all these plants so fast and to remember their names. I found other things that were identified in a pamphlet we carried on the walk. In the bog area, just off the boardwalk, I saw bog rosemary, marsh (!!&%$%@@@ Danny) marigolds, bog bean, buck bean and tamarack trees. On the way out, near a lookout tower, I saw fireweed, Solomon's seal and wild roses. But no matter how hard I looked, I didn't see any orchids.

I asked Paul if he had seen any orchids on this walk, and he said, "Just one," and then when I asked him where it was, he sort of laughed. I don't know what he meant by that. When people say things I don't understand, then I really feel like I'm in the dark, and even writing it down here doesn't help much. Maybe he was teasing me and really didn't see any orchids. That's probably what Shauna would have said. Probably I should have laughed, too, but I didn't think of it at the time.

Shauna taught me so many things. I like to think of her as a translator. Not that I don't speak English, but sometimes I feel that the English I speak is a different language from everyone else's English. In the classroom, with so much noise and activity, it's especially hard to understand things. I can't pick up the same signals as other people. It's like being in a room with ten TVs on all at once, and I know there are words around, but I can't isolate any meanings from them. Shauna could help me tune in to the right signal. I wonder if I will ever see her again. She told me that she would write me a postcard, but I haven't gotten one yet.

I am starting to think that Shauna is not my friend. She has not written me a postcard, and she said she would. If I do not get a postcard from her by Friday, I will know she is not my friend. If she does write me, I will write her back and ask about signals from boys and what to do if I can't hear them and also what to do if I can.

I did not see any snakes on the trail. After the walk, the naturalists drove us back in their vans and dropped us off at the nature center. I went to Danny's pizza place—I can't get used to calling it Pizza Penny's—and had lunch with Mom. She asked about the walk, but while I was identifying the names of all the plants I saw and naming the other ones from the pamphlet, she asked me to stop and talk about something else. I find that very irritating, when people ask you about something and then after a while tell you they don't want you to talk about it anymore. People shouldn't ask in the first place if they don't want the answer.

How I Met a Boy and Talked to Him

I felt tired after lunch, so I went and lay on my bed. Mom was working her shift in the kitchen, and so I had to plan the rest of the day on my own. I decided that first I would go and walk on the beach, and then I would go and visit the nature center again. I walked down the beach, had a swing and then headed up the hill through the woods, only to find that the door was locked. On the sign it said that the nature center closes at two o'clock on Sundays. I will try to remember that.

Maybe it was because I was tired, but when I discovered that the nature center was closed, I got tears in my eyes. I do not like a change of plans. I stood at the door and tried to think of what to do next. It was hot and I hadn't brought my hat. Sometimes, when things aren't what I expect I get this whirly feeling. I had it then. I felt the sun burning the back of my neck. Suddenly, I heard a voice behind me.

"Hey, you're new around here, aren't you?"

I spun around. A boy was standing behind me wearing navy swimming trunks and carrying a volleyball. His legs were tanned and looked as if he had spent a lot of time out in the sun. I looked up briefly at his head and noticed that he had short, spiked brown hair streaked with blond.

I had trouble deciding how to answer him. We arrived two days ago, but this was my third day here, so I wasn't as new as I could have been. I decided to give him a specific answer about when I had arrived.

"We arrived on Friday," I said.

He grinned.

"Hey, so did I. But I've been up every weekend since the first of May. My aunt and uncle have a cabin here. You?"

Now that I see this written here, I know what he was asking. He was wondering where I was staying. At the time, I couldn't figure out his meaning from the word, "You?" and so I just started walking. There was a path down from the nature center toward the beach, and I took it.

"Do you want to go for a walk?" he asked from behind me.

"I am walking," I said and kept on going, but I'm not sure if he heard me as I think I was mumbling. He didn't follow, and I heard him bouncing the volleyball on the stone walk in front of the nature center. You're not supposed to dribble volleyballs. Basketballs are for dribbling.

I wonder if he wants to be my boyfriend. He looks like he's a few years younger than me, but that's okay. Everyone I went to school with was younger. That's because I spent an extra year in Kindergarten to work on my social skills.

I remember asking about why I was staying another year in Kindergarten when everyone else in my class was going on to grade one, and that's just what my mother told me—that it was to work on my social skills. I could already read, and most of the other kids couldn't, so I thought somebody had made a mistake when I had failed and they hadn't. I hated school when I was young because I wasn't used to the routine. Deep down, I did want to go, but I wished intensely that the other kids weren't there.

My mom came and sat on my bed just now and asked what I'd been up to today. I started telling her about the nature center walk and the plants I'd seen, and she said, "No, no, don't go into all that again. I just want to know what else you've been up to." She had that H on her forehead. She'll have to look out, or someday those wrinkles will stick like that.

I wanted to tell her about the boy who had talked to me, but I couldn't. Instead I started to cry. I wish I looked like Sandra Bullock when I'm crying, but I think I don't. Mom rubbed my back and said it was okay, and that I was getting used to a lot of new things. When I stopped crying, she asked if I'd like to go shopping with her tomorrow and look at some of the summer clothing. I said I didn't want to look at any !!&%$%@@@ summer clothing, and then she said don't swear and that she'd like me to think about buying something summery. She said my jean dress was fine, but it looked hot, and she'd noticed I had a pizza stain on it. I got up and grabbed the dress and took it down to the washroom and scrubbed out the stain. She can try and make me shop for new clothes, but she can't make me wear them.

I hope if I just lie here and listen to my clock ticking I will stop whirling inside my head. The fact that the passing of time is regular and inevitable is very reassuring. Not like meeting boys, who are not inevitable, but who I know are out there, having just met one. The thing I need to know is this: Is the boy I met here the one for me?

Monday July 1
How a Boy Asked Me to a Dance Some Other Time

I started the day in a similar fashion to yesterday, eating breakfast (three pancakes) at the same table I ate at before and then going for a walk on the beach. The fact that I went up and down the beach seven times was private, and nobody has to know about it, except me. I got to the nature center at ten, just when Paul was unlocking the door. His hands are very brown. You can see golden hairs along the fingers.

"I forgot to ask you what your last name was," I said. "I know that your first name is Paul because I saw it on your name tag, but you must have a last name because everybody does and I want to know it. Names are extremely important."

I liked how he listened and didn't try to rush me.

"It's Jacobs," he said. "My wife likes it because her name is June, and June Jacobs has a nice ring."

"June Jacobs has a nice ring," I repeated. I think he meant that the sound of the name was nice, not that she had on a ring. Although she probably does have on a ring if she's married.

46

I said, "I had a gerbil named June. We bought her in June. That's why we called her that."

Paul opened a cabinet and took out food for the fish that were swimming in a big tank. They made me nervous because I know they are fish from the lake, and I started to think about people swimming in the lake with them and how one of the people might be me, swimming against my will.

"Gerbils are nocturnal," I said, "and they make good pets, even though they scramble about a lot at night and make lots of noise and sometimes wake you up when you're sleeping, but if you're not sleeping, then they are good company."

"June is good company, too," said Paul and laughed. "Must be the name."

"My first name is Taylor and my last name is Simon. I use it even though it's my dad's, and he doesn't live with us anymore. He lives in Cody, Wyoming."

"Do you see him much?" Paul asked.

"No. He left when I was eight."

There was a little silence, and then Paul said, "My dad left when I was eight, too."

I could tell by his hands that he wanted to say something more. When people want to keep talking their hands keep moving.

"Did he go to Wyoming?" I asked.

"Nope. He died."

"Oh," I said. "Being dead is just as bad as being away."

"Depends on your perspective," said Paul, grinning. I wasn't sure what he meant at first, but then I figured it out. If you're the person who is away, it probably isn't as bad as being dead.

"Unless, if it's you, and you really don't want to be away," I said, smiling to let him know that I understood. "If that is the case, being away is just as bad as being dead."

"True," he said.

"How did he die?"

Paul pushed up his sleeves with his hands and folded them carefully at the cuffs.

"He killed himself."

"Oh," I said. I wanted to ask him more about how his dad had died, but I wasn't sure I should. Some questions can be too personal. I wondered if he might be feeling sad about his father being dead.

"Would you like to be left alone?" I said.

"No," said Paul. "No problem. Today is a new day."

This statement is confusing. Every day is a new day. How could you have a day that is old, unless it is yesterday and you are going back to it. But traveling in reverse is impossible unless you are on a number line and you go into negative numbers, but you can only do this in math and only in your head.

"Do you have any children?" I asked.

"Nope, but we have a cat," he said.

"I like cats," I said. "I have heard that cats are autistic dogs."

"Oh," said Paul. "I hadn't heard that one. But you might have something there."

I think what he meant by this was that I might have a point. I looked down at my hands when he said it, though, just in case, but they were empty.

"Are you going to transplant any more bog specimens today?" I asked.

"Nope, we'll leave the others alone so tourists can see them. Most people who come to the park don't care much about the flora and fauna, and just come to water ski and party. Wish they'd do those things somewhere else. For the few that do care, we try to keep the trails fresh."

"How many trails are there?" I asked.

"Eight. Nine if you count Kingsmere, but it's closed right now on account of bears."

"I know they wouldn't be panda bears," I said.

"Black bears," Paul chuckled. "Don't see many pandas this far from China."

Paul unlocked another cabinet and took out bottles. Each bottle was full of a different animal's poop, and people were supposed to guess the animal by its droppings. I picked up the black bear's and studied it for a moment. You could see berries in it. I kept looking at the jar and tried not to look at the fish in the aquarium.

"The panda isn't actually a bear, you know," I said. "It was first described by Père David, a French missionary. He was also the first one to describe the Mongolian gerbil. That was the kind of gerbil I had."

"June?"

"June, Charlotte, Walnut and Hammy. Hammy was the last one. My suitcase smells like him."

"Oh," Paul said.

"The Mongolian gerbil's Latin name is *Meriones unguiculatus*. *Meriones* was also the name of a Greek soldier in Homer's *Iliad*. *Unguiculatus* means 'with fingernails.'"

Paul chuckled again.

"Did your gerbils ever scratch you?"

"Lots of times. But they didn't mean to; they were just scared."

"Funny, you don't look very threatening."

"I'm not," I said.

After I finished visiting the nature center, I went back home for lunch, and then my mom's shift was done and we walked down the beach to the Canada Day festivities. I didn't examine any of the displays, except for the environmental booth, where I won a Clean Water T-shirt. It's way too big, but Mom says it will look good over top a bathing suit. I do not wear a bathing suit, however, because I do not swim, so I probably won't have much opportunity to wear the T-shirt.

Swimming is an unhygienic activity. I don't understand why anyone would want to hang around in water that other people have been in. And fish. And other wildlife. Imagine inviting other people and animals and a few fish to join you in the bathtub. This thought makes me sick.

This evening, we had supper and then Mom had to work again. I could hear music playing from down the street, and I walked a few blocks to the hall, which is across the road from the nature center, and listened to the music for a while. It was much nicer listening from a distance because it was too loud when I went close. It wasn't classical baroque, which was disappointing.

A boy from the beach biked past, and I knew it was the same one who had talked to me earlier because he had the same spiked hair. After he passed, he turned and came back toward me on the sidewalk. He was wearing blue jeans and a white T-shirt.

"Hey, Beautiful, going to the dance?" he asked.

"No," I said because I wasn't.

"Want to go with me?" he said.

"No," I said again. This was being truthful because I don't like loud music. Dances would be fine if it wasn't for the music. Now that I see it written here, my two no's were not a good attempt at conversation. When he speaks to me again, I will try to talk more. He looked really good in the blue jeans.

"Okay, well, maybe some other time," he said and pushed his bike back onto the street. "See you 'round."

I nodded. Nodding is just as good as speaking, sometimes, and at least I didn't say no a third time. No, no, no, no. There, that's seven, and hopefully I can relax now and go to sleep.

I wonder when he will ask me to another dance. Does planning to ask me to a dance mean we are dating?

Note to self: Boyfriend is defined as a person's regular male companion or lover. I have not crossed over and achieved this goal, but I think I'm on my way.

Tuesday July 2
A Nature Center Walk in the Absence of Boys

It was ten past twelve the final time I looked at my clock last night. I read over the best pages from my *Oxford English Dictionary* to try and relax, but it didn't work. Then I woke up at seven with a squirrel chattering outside my window. When I looked outside, I saw it on a branch of a tree, and for a minute, I thought it was Hammy. The squirrel was the same color as my gerbils—it's called agouti, sort of a mixture of light and dark colored fur. My potential boyfriend has hair like that.

I wish I were better at remembering faces. I am not sure I will recognize this boy again if I see him on the street. It would be important to acknowledge him if I see him again, by saying, "Hey," or, "What's new?" or some other piece of small talk to let him know I care. It's going to be hard to do this, however, if I don't know which boy he is.

I asked my mom at breakfast how she goes about recognizing her boyfriends, and she laughed and said it was easy.

"If it were easy," I said, "I'd know how to do it."

"Well, you've got to concentrate on a feature or two that is really unique," she said.

"Uh-huh. Like a golf shirt," I said.

"No, Taylor, not like anything they're wearing. Two people could have the same clothes, but not be the same person."

"Well, what should you concentrate on?"

"The twinkle in their eye, maybe, or the way they have a dimple in their cheek. You've got to scan a person's face and put it all together in a picture, the same way you do other things you look at."

This is going to be very hard, I thought. But if it's too hard, then maybe I'm never going to grow up and that would be unbearable. Imagine being a child forever. My grandmother says, "No pain, no gain." I don't like my grandmother, but I think this slogan is correct, and I'm not going to give up on boys, regardless of how hard it is to meet one.

After breakfast, I went walking and then to the nature center. It's getting to be a nice routine that I'm comfortable with—first the walking, then the nature center. Since it opens at ten, I'm often the only one there for a while, and it's quiet and calm. The girl behind the counter is usually reading a novel because there are no customers. I want to sing out, "Somewhere Over the Rainbow," when I see her because she still reminds me of Dorothy in *The Wizard of Oz*, but I contain myself. People look at you funny when you do things like sing in front of them. Singing in public is only acceptable in movies, unless you are a paid singer and you are giving a concert.

Today, Paul was cutting out leaves for people to print things on and attach to a cardboard tree that was propped in the entranceway. He asked if I wanted to help, but I'm no good at cutting so I just watched. Paul wasn't wearing his Indiana Jones hat, and his hair is fairly long and very shiny and clean. Looking at it made me think about Danny and how his oily fingerprints had gotten onto my map and probably worked their way into my pockets where I've been putting my hands. I looked around to see if there was any place I could wash, and there wasn't. This made me a bit upset. Then I started thinking about printing swear words on the leaves, and I had a hard time not writing !!&%$%@@@ on a leaf and pinning it up. Once an idea like this gets into my head, it's a struggle not to act on it. I think I must be getting better prevention muscles because I managed not to give in to the urge.

"Did you know that the CIA once trained gerbils to work as secret agents?" I said to Paul.

"Huh, really," he said. "That's an interesting thought."

"Gerbils have a really strong sense of smell," I said, "and the CIA trained them to identify people who were sweaty. The gerbils were used in airports, and they would press a lever to get food if they sensed someone with elevated adrenalin. The only trouble was that people who were afraid of flying, or had other problems, also had raised adrenaline—the same as people who were breaking the law, so the gerbils identified more people than the CIA's true targets."

Paul seemed really impressed by this information and listened to all of it without telling me not to talk so much about gerbils. I appreciated that.

At the end, though, he said, "Well, isn't that the rat's rubbers." I didn't know what he could be talking about because I was referring to gerbils, not rats. And everybody knows rats don't wear boots . . . so I guess this must be one of those phrases that people use when they really mean something else. It's stupid not to say what you mean.

By the time I was finished talking, a bunch of people had come in, and when I noticed this, I'm sure my adrenaline went up. I discovered in a magazine that it's the adrenaline in your body that makes you feel hyper if you're anxious. I chewed some gum and walked around to the back of the center to give myself room away from them, but some of the kids followed me and one asked if there were any puppets.

"I don't know," I said.

"Taylor, the puppets are in the cupboard under the window," Paul called. He must have heard the child's question. "Would you mind taking them out? I haven't had time, yet."

I went and opened the drawers of the cupboard and took out the puppets. The children tried them on and made up little puppet shows with each other.

"What do you eat?" a crow asked a black bear.

"Berries and seeds. And kangaroos," said the black bear.

I smiled to myself. Kids don't know very much.

After a few minutes, I saw a bunch of books with wild plants in them, and I read for a while. Then one of the women came by and asked me about the bog specimens that were in the aquarium right beside me.

"What are they called?" she asked.

I didn't know what she was talking about at first.

"Those," she said.

I tried hard to follow her eye gaze, something that I have practiced a great deal in the past.

"The big one is the pitcher plant," I said. "See the leaves? Inside, the water in them traps the insects." I told her about the other plants, too, pointing out each one as I spoke. She said that they had seen some of the plants on their walk yesterday.

"We have another walk this afternoon," Paul called out. "It's the Tea Pail Trail. We have some cars leaving here at two, or you can meet us there."

"Well, if it doesn't rain, I'll probably come," the woman said and told the children to put away the puppets. "I'm just babysitting them, and this afternoon, I won't have anything better to do."

I thought about going on the trail, too, and decided that I would.

"Well, if it doesn't rain, I'll probably come," I said to Paul when I left for lunch.

"See you then," he answered.

At lunch, my mother told me that I had been here four days without ever having eaten a vegetable. She made me order a small salad to go with my french fries. I couldn't eat it because I couldn't sleep last night. When I'm tired, things that normally seem bad seem worse, like salad. "Potatoes are vegetables," I said, but like usual she wasn't paying attention. Just to test her out, I said quietly, "Potatoes are !!&%$%@@@ mammals," and she just nodded and put another package of sugar in her coffee. Sugar and coffee are two things that can kill you. Along with cigarettes.

This essay is really long, but I want to tell about the nature walk. It's only nine o'clock, and if I write for another twenty minutes and then take ten minutes to get to sleep (ha-ha, wishful thinking) and wake up at eight, then I will have had ten and a half hours of sleep. If I take forty minutes to get to sleep, which is much more likely, then I will have had ten hours of sleep.

I met Paul and Julie, the other naturalist, at the nature center and got a ride to the trail with Julie. She has shoulder-length dark hair. She also has a big mark on one of her arms that is like a blister. I know I'm not supposed to stare at it. A girl at my school had a stained arm from a fire because someone was smoking at her house. I wonder when Julie's house burned down.

When she got into the driver's seat, she had difficulty doing up her seatbelt.

"Boy, I'm getting fat," she said. "Gotta get back on that diet."

"I don't think you are fat," I said. "You fit in your clothes."

The Tea Pail Trail has boardwalk around most of it, and you walk single file along the boardwalk looking at the plants that grow alongside. As everyone walked, I scanned each person to see if there were any boys my age, but there were not. Maybe nature trails are not the best places to meet a boy. I have heard that bars are a good place to meet boys, but I don't know where the bars are here, and anyway, I don't enjoy drinking.

The woman babysitting the children did come to walk the trail. She let Paul tell her the names of all the flowers we saw. She said he sure knew a lot and that he must have a very good memory. I knew all the names of the flowers, too. I did not see any orchids, although I looked for them. I did see lots of the plants I've learned to identify from reading identification books at the nature center. When I saw the false dandelion, it was so yellow I felt like sneezing. I told Paul and he laughed. I'm not sure why.

As we walked down the boardwalk, one of the people—a large man in a Hawaiian shirt—reached over and picked three of the Solomon's seal plants.

"This is a national park," said Paul. "Please, no flower picking."

"I'm just picking a few," the man said. It sounded to me like he was talking back.

Then a bunch of the kids started picking flowers, too, and Paul had to stop them. After that, the babysitter took her dog off its leash, and the dog ran ahead and left droppings along the trail. Paul told her to put the dog back on the leash. It must be exhausting trying to control other people and their dogs.

We stopped by the bridge, and Paul told the group that rose petals are edible; you just lay them out on a cookie sheet, sprinkle them with sugar and bake them at a very low temperature for a half hour. I might ask if I can bake some in the restaurant kitchen when they're not too busy making other things. As we walked away, I saw the large man reach out and grab some rose petals and stuff them into his mouth. I can't be sure, but it looked as though his mouth had more than the usual two rows of teeth. Like a shark's jaws.

I leaned over the railing of the bridge and looked into the water. I saw fish gliding past through the weeds, and there were tall plants called cattails growing in clumps along the water's edge. One of the kids started throwing rocks down into the water at the fish and scared them away.

"Live and let live," said Paul.

We moved on, and Paul told the group that you can dig the cattail root and dry it and grind it into flour. It tastes, he said, like arrowroot.

"I used to eat arrowroot cookies when I was small," I said to Paul when he came and stood beside me. "I think something in the arrowroot has a calming effect."

"I could use some of that right now," he said, and I knew what he meant. It's funny nobody markets cattail flour. I'm sure health food addicts would want to buy it. Better than tranquilizers, any day.

I think the pills they put me on when I was eight might have been tranquilizers. I can't remember the name on the bottle. They made me feel as though I wanted to sit down all the time, but when I sat down, I immediately wanted to get up. I can remember feeling relaxed on the outside, but jumpy on the inside. Then for a while I wished I was dead, and I must have talked about it because my mom took me off the !!&%$%@@@ pills. Later on, I heard that this medication had never been tested on children, although it was prescribed a lot. That's pretty stupid, if you ask me. But humans do stupid things all the time.

The other thing that I saw growing along the trail was a plant called Labrador tea. The aboriginal people used to dry the leaves and make tea. Paul said that later in the summer, they would have a tea-making class at the nature center, and I would be welcome to come.

The reason the trail got its name is because there is an old camp near the highway where a bunch of rusty pails are half buried in an area that used to be a dump. Someone took one and hung it on a tree branch, as a reminder that time has passed, Paul said, since the olden days when people camped here.

I don't mind thinking about the past passing, but I don't like thinking about the future coming. The Future. I can see myself standing on the edge of a cliff that drops off into night.

Wednesday July 3
Double Sighting: Orchids and the Potential Boyfriend

A kid at the nature center asked me what day it was this morning, and I told her it was Wednesday. I know that it's Wednesday because I counted the days this morning. Two more days until I get a postcard from Shauna, if she is still my friend.

Before the kid asked me what day it was, she asked the girl who works behind the counter. The girl's name is Rose. She did not know what day it was. The kid wanted to know because she was writing in the guest book and had to put down the date of her visit. I was glad I could help her.

Rose acts like she's busy all the time, but really I don't think she does very much. A lot of people come to look at the books, but they act bored and not many buy one. Rose always wears her hair in braids, and today she had little beads woven through the braids.

"What trail has the most orchids?" I asked Paul. He nodded and I think this meant that he was glad I had asked. He said that it was getting a bit late in the season for orchids, but because we had a cold spring there might still be a chance. He said that there hadn't been a sighting yet as far as he knew and that he was going to go out around the outdoor theater this morning for a look.

"A sighting," said Rose. "I saw something last year over the lake that would beat the petals off of one of your orchids."

"What?" I asked.

"Aliens," she said. "I didn't have my EMF Detector with me, but I could feel the electricity in the air."

"Maybe it was lightning," said Paul. "You could have seen sheet lightning if there was a storm."

"There wasn't a storm," said Rose. "Something was up there, and I think it was trying to land. It eventually just disappeared, though. I keep looking and maybe I'll see it again. Next time, I hope I have a camera with me."

"Good luck," said Paul and laughed. I wondered what an EMF Detector was, but I didn't have time to ask. I was busy thinking about Rose's perspective and how it was different from mine. I don't believe in aliens.

"Want to come?" Paul said.

"Come where?" I was still thinking about the aliens.

"To the outdoor theater. See if we can find an orchid or two."

"What's the outdoor theater?"

"It's a stage where there are shows about Prince Albert National Park."

"About Waskesiu, you mean?"

"Yes," he said.

"Okay, I'll come," I said.

A couple of bikes were leaning up against the inside wall of the back room, and he helped me carry mine outside. I hoped it

61

would be okay for me to ride it, and I wondered whose it was. When I asked, Paul got quiet for a minute, and I thought maybe he didn't know. Then he said that it was June's.

"June the wife, not June the gerbil," I said. He laughed.

The outdoor theater is near the campground. There is a wide stage with lamps along the front. On Friday and Saturday nights, the naturalists—the people like Paul who study the plants and animals here and share information with visitors—put on shows. I will see if Mom would like to go to a show. She sometimes likes to go to live theater in Saskatoon, like when *A Chorus Line* or *Fame* comes to town. Paul said their shows weren't like those ones, but I can't imagine exactly what they will be like. Maybe he meant that they'll be shorter.

Some people are good at thinking about things they have never seen. I am not. I need to see something once before I can get a picture in my head. That's why thinking about The Future is so scary for me—because I really can't imagine it at all. In the fall I will have all these empty days stretching out, and I am supposed to fill them up. I can't go back to high school because I have finished all my courses. I wish I had failed grade twelve English, and then I could have gone back and taken it again. I would have liked to repeat Mrs. Thomson's English class.

My mother thinks I should take a cooking class. She says it would be easy for me to get a job in a restaurant if I took a cooking class. The important fact related to this is that I hate cooking. My grandmother thinks I should go to university. She says I am very smart. I have been to the university a few times, and I know that if I could get lost in my high school, which I did, I for sure would get lost at the university. Also, my grandmother is not right about everything. She tried to get me to play chess for the longest time. She says that people with autism are good at chess. I think chess sucks.

I know that lots of people my age are getting summer jobs. I am too afraid to apply for a job. You wouldn't know what questions the person would ask you, and so there would be no way to prepare. You also wouldn't know exactly what you'd be doing, and it would be freaky to go to work without really knowing what you'd have to do. Just thinking about it makes me !!&%$%@@@ sick to my stomach.

Anyway, when I was poking around near the parking lot, I spotted an orchid! It was a yellow lady's slipper, and Paul said this was a very good discovery. I was very glad I found it, except for the fact that it was yellow. *Cypripedium parviflorum* is its Latin name.

"It's not too late!" I said. "Orchids are still in season!" Paul asked if I'd like to fill out a rare plant report back at the nature center, and I said I would. On the way back, we biked past the boy that might want to be my boyfriend. He was wearing jeans and a white T-shirt, and I recognized him even though I thought I wouldn't. He waved at me when we passed, and I waved back.

When we stopped biking, Paul asked if that was my boyfriend back there. I said no, I didn't have a boyfriend, which is true because he hasn't kissed me yet.

Paul asked what I was waiting for, and I didn't know what to say.

"Christmas?" he said, and I nodded. Then I felt stupid. Why would I say I was waiting for Christmas? There's no guarantee that you'll get a boyfriend for Christmas.

I suppose I could have said, "I'm waiting for that boy to come and talk to me again," but it didn't seem quite right to say that. I was thinking also that I was actually waiting for five to twelve, because I was getting hungry, and five to twelve is the time I go back to the restaurant for lunch. That answer didn't really go with his question, though. Making conversation with people can be hard. I shifted topics. I asked why June never came to the nature center, and Paul said that June was in a wheelchair and felt too sorry for herself to come out unless it was dark and people couldn't see her. I asked how she'd gotten into the wheelchair, and he said she had a disease called multiple sclerosis that made her muscles weak.

"Will she ever walk again?" I asked.

"I don't know," he said. "It depends if she goes into a remission."

"Is there anything she can do to help herself go into a remission?" I asked.

"Think happy thoughts," he said. "Which is a Catch-22 because how can you think happy thoughts when all you want to do is walk and you can't."

"Once, my mom and dad had a big fight, and my dad drove me around and around. We went past the pet store two times. On the third time, we didn't go past, but we went in, and I asked for a cat. My dad said no. I asked for other pets. He said no. I asked for a gerbil. He said yes, and we bought a gerbil and took it home. That was my first gerbil. His name was Walnut."

"Is that what you think about when you want to be happy?" Paul asked.

"Yes, it is," I said. "Maybe June could get a gerbil." Paul looked at his hands for a minute.

"Maybe," he said. "But our cat would probably eat it." Then he took a package of cigarettes out of his shirt pocket and put one in his mouth.

"You're not going to smoke?" I said.

"I was planning to," said Paul.

"Cigarettes cause cancer. They're very bad for you. If you want to be healthy, you shouldn't smoke," I told him. He said if the smoking bothered me, he'd wait until later. But that bothers me, too. You shouldn't smoke at any time. Paul is not a good person anymore because he smokes.

Multiple sclerosis must be a disease like cancer. I'm glad that all I have is Asperger's Syndrome and not a disease. It must be terrible to have weak muscles and not know if you'll get better or worse. Or with cancer, to know that you will get worse and worse until you die. Unless you get cured. I have very good health, except for colds. It's good to try and stay away from germs if you can. When Mom's boyfriends come to the house, I think about how many germs they might have touched during the day and brought back to us. You can use multiplication to predict the results. Like if a boyfriend visits for twelve days and each day he brings in fourteen germs, there are 168 germs in all.

When I was leaving the nature center, I saw two trucks pull up in front of the hall across the street. People started unloading boxes and some furniture. I wonder what they were doing. They couldn't be moving in there because it's not a house. They sure had a lot of stuff, though.

They even had a bed. Why would they have a bed unless there's a bedroom?

Thursday July 4
The Change of Plans That Had a Boy in It

After I finished writing last night, my mother came in and crushed a spider on the window ledge. Then she sat on my bed. She was mad because I haven't been spending much time with her. This doesn't make sense to me because she told me to fend for myself. I should have tried to build a bridge with words when she accused me of isolating myself, but instead I got mad.

"I don't want to go !!&%$%@@@ shopping," I said.

"Stop swearing! Can't we have a conversation without you swearing?" she said. "It doesn't have to be shopping. We can do other things. Like maybe tomorrow (which is today) we could go to a movie."

"Do you know how many different types of flowers grow around here?" I asked. I had been planning to tell her about finding the orchid, but she interrupted me.

"Stop changing the subject. We are talking about movies," said Mom. "If you want to ask a question, ask a question about movies."

"What is that Indiana Jones movie called? The one with the snakes?"

"Why?" asked Mom.

"Because I don't like snakes."

"Not that kind of question. Try again," she said.

"What movies are playing?" I asked, thinking of saying *!!&%$%@@@ movies,* but restraining myself.

"We could go check it out," she said. "But it doesn't matter what movies are playing. If two people want to spend time together and go to a movie, they'll make the best of whatever's on. It's being together that matters, not the actual movie."

"But what if the only movies are stupid?" I asked. "Then do the people go to them anyway?"

"Sometimes, and they can sit together and make fun of the movie."

This doesn't make sense to me. Why would people go to a movie they know they won't like?

After this conversation, Mom went off and wrote down stuff about going to the movies. Then she came back and handed me the sheet of paper for my binder.

"Where is your binder?" she asked.

"What binder?" I said, not meaning to make her mad, but stalling for time so that I could think of an alibi regarding my binder.

"Your social stories binder," she said. "You don't mean to tell me that you've forgotten it!"

"I didn't forget it."

"Then where is it?"

"I just didn't want to bring it. It had food on the cover."

"Oh Taylor, those stories can be really helpful for you."

"But I know them already," I said. "And now that I'm done school, it's juvenile to drag around a binder. . . ."

Mom paused. "Okay," she said. "Okay, but keep this sheet about movies somewhere safe. You never know when you might need to read it again."

I rolled it up and put it inside one of my sandals.

So then we made a plan to go to a movie this afternoon. I was supposed to come back to the restaurant for lunch, and then we would check out the movies and decide which one we were going to see. When I came out of the nature center, though, I had a change of plans. I ran into the boy again. I forget his name, but I know it starts with a K. He was wearing his navy swimming trunks and a red and blue shirt, and sitting on the bench outside the nature center. When I came out and saw him, I went over and sat down. I had been thinking about him, and I was thinking that if you want someone to be your boyfriend, you'd better talk to him.

When I sat down, he said, "Hi," and I said, "Hi." Then I said, "Do you want to be my boyfriend?" and he laughed. Then he said he'd thought maybe I was shy, but now he knew I wasn't and he was glad.

He told me he's from Regina, and he's staying up here at his aunt and uncle's cabin while his parents have gone fishing farther north.

"Are your aunt and uncle home?" I asked.

"Sometimes, but not all the time," he said. "Do you want to come over and hang out? We could grab some lunch on the way."

"Okay," I said. I felt really good that he wanted to have lunch just with me. So that's when the change of plans started. It felt funny being the one to invent the change of plans. Usually other people change the plans and then tell me about it.

We walked to a burger place, and he ordered while I sat on the deck and thought about all the plants I've seen up here so far. I wanted to tell him about them, but I wasn't sure if I should just start talking about them or if I should wait until he asked. Good thing I decided to wait because when he came back with the burgers and we'd walked for a while, he said he liked it that I was kind of quiet.

"You're kind of quiet, too," I said, and he laughed.

"Why don't you ever look at me when I talk to you?" he said.

"Why would I look at you when I know where you are?" I answered, and he laughed again. I thought that things were going very well, judging by all the laughing.

We went into his aunt and uncle's cabin, and he set the food on the table. I thought we were going to eat it right away, but he said, "Do you want to eat now or just hang out first?"

I wasn't sure what he meant by hang out, but I wasn't hungry, and anyway, I don't eat hamburgers.

"We could hang out," I said. He showed me around the cabin and it was very small and then I sat on the couch and he sat beside me.

"Do you really want a boyfriend?" he asked.

He was sitting kind of close, and I got this smothery feeling, like I do when people are in my personal space, but I said yeah. Then he moved right over and kissed me on the mouth. I jumped back. People can have lots of germs in their saliva. I wiped my face with my sleeve.

"Hey, what's wrong?" he said. "I thought you said you wanted to."

"I found a !!&%$%@@@ yellow lady's slipper near the outdoor theater," I blurted. "Lady's slippers are orchids. The white ones are pretty rare, some are extinct, and I bet not many people up here have seen them," I went on. "The yellow lady's slippers have been used as herbs for medicines to counteract insomnia and anxiety. Their Latin name is *Cypripdium parviflorum*."

He stood up and got his hamburger and I kept talking about lady's slippers some more and then about the other flowers I've seen and he asked me if I was going to eat my hamburger and I said no, that I didn't like hamburgers, and he said, "Well, what did you make me buy it for?" and I decided it was time to go and I left. I'm not sure if he is my boyfriend, and if he is, I'm not sure I like it.

When I got back to the restaurant, it was nearly two o'clock, and Mom had the H in her forehead and said she was very mad and asked if I was trying to drive her crazy and I said no I wasn't, but she didn't believe me because she kept on telling me how worried she had been and that now it was too late to go to the movies, even though we hadn't found out exactly what time the movies were or even what their names were, and I started to cry and Mom asked if I had eaten anything.

"No," I said. "Someone, maybe my boyfriend, bought me a hamburger, but I didn't want it."

"Who bought you a hamburger?" Mom asked, and when I told her that I couldn't remember his name, she had all sorts of questions, like where had I met him and what kind of a boy was he. I didn't know how to answer any of the questions because I couldn't remember exactly where I had talked to him first, and in terms of what kind of a boy he was, I didn't know what to say to that, but I tried.

"He has agouti hair," I said.

"Just answer the question!"

"I am answering the !!&%$%@@@ question!" I said. "He's a little shorter than me," I went on. "He has curly hair and I don't know what color his eyes are and he usually wears navy track pants or swimming trunks and a T-shirt, sometimes white, sometimes red and blue. And runners. And I've seen him in blue jeans. And he's maybe a ten."

After twenty more questions, she said that if I was going to have a change of plans again, I should call her and let her know. Then she wrote down the number of the restaurant on a piece of paper and put it in my purse, got me a plate of pancakes and went to lie down. I started thinking about the questions she had asked me and thought about what I'd have said if she had asked them about Paul. I thought it was funny that I knew all the answers when they were about Paul, like his name is Paul Jacobs and he is interested in plants and animals and he has a sick wife and he is a good listener. But Paul is a bad person because he smokes.

A Change of Plans with a Play in It

Thinking of Mom's questions gave me a headache, and so I brushed my teeth because of the kissing germs and then lay down and watched my clock for a while. It seems to me that you should know the answers to the kinds of questions Mom was asking if you have a boyfriend.

I tried hard and finally I remembered his name. It is Kody.

I wonder if Kody likes me as much as I like him, which isn't much, or if maybe he likes me more. I hope he doesn't think I am dumb or guess that I have special needs. It shouldn't matter whether a person has special needs or not, if someone really likes you. Paul's wife has special needs, and he still likes her.

I had two orders of fries for supper because I was still hungry even after the pancakes. Mom let me eat them because she had to start her shift and she wasn't responsible for my table. Everything we order just goes on our tab, and I don't know if Mom pays it or not or if it comes off her salary or if Danny just tears it up because he's her boyfriend.

I didn't feel tired or like staying in my room, so I went out for a walk. I walked seven times up and down the beach and looked at the little kids playing in the playground. Then I walked around town. I looked at the map once or twice, so I wouldn't get lost, and ended up by the nature center, which was closed, of course. Across the street, the lights were on in the hall and the door was open. There was a sandwich board sign out front saying Pinter Festival. I went over and read the small print on the poster, which said that the play tonight started at eight o'clock. It was written by Harold Pinter, and there would be other plays by the same playwright, running at different times, so that's probably why it's called a festival. I had half an hour until the play started, so I went inside and asked a girl at a table if they still had tickets, and she said they did, and then I asked if I could use the phone, and she gave me her cell phone. I called Mom at the restaurant and said that I had another change of plans and that I was going to go to this play tonight, if that was okay with her.

"Two changes of plans in one day!" she said. "That's quite unusual! Does this change of plans have to do with this nameless boy?"

"He's not a nameless boy," I said. "His name is Kody."

"Uh-huh," said Mom. "What's his last name?"

"Wyoming," I said, although I know it probably isn't.

"Very funny," she said. "Taylor, are you making up all of this? All the business about this boy?" Her voice sounded like she had the H in her forehead.

"No, I'm not," I said. "By the way, I have to go because the play is going to start." Then I clicked End on the cell phone.

I gave the girl back her phone and bought a ticket. Then I went and sat down. I like to be in an aisle seat exactly halfway between the front and the back. There were fifteen rows, so it was difficult to decide where the middle was—I could have chosen either row seven or eight. I picked seven, for obvious reasons.

I read through the program and saw that there would be three acts and that the playwright, Harold Pinter, was British. The play was quite short—each act took only about twenty minutes—and it was very complicated. The main character's name was Stanley. I didn't understand much of the story, but the parts I did understand sent chills down my spine, and that made up for not understanding the other parts. I haven't seen anything like this play before. When it was done, I sat almost shaking in my seat—that's how good it was.

The way the characters spoke to each other was so interesting. I could see the lessons that Shauna taught me about conversations right up there on the stage. For one thing, people repeated what each other said. Someone would say, "I didn't sleep at all," and the other person would say, "You didn't sleep at all?" Shauna practiced this with me a lot. She said it was one of the ways the Queen uses to keep a conversation going, by engaging people in talking about their interests.

The people talking in the play reminded me of other things Shauna taught me about having a conversation. For example, the actors waited, sometimes for quite a while, after someone spoke. In real communication, you're supposed to pause so that you look as if you're really listening to what the person has said. The pauses in the play gave me a chance to process what was being said. If they had gone any faster, I would have had trouble catching on.

There were lots of times that people changed the topic during a conversation, too; it's okay to do this, as long as you think the first topic is finished. As I listened, though, I thought that some of the changes in topic were jerky, as if the person shouldn't have changed topics so suddenly. I wonder if I do this? I will have to listen to myself in conversations to see if I do this.

I could really relate to the part when the person said he didn't sleep. Sometimes, I don't sleep either, although I have slept better up here in Waskesiu than I would have expected. Maybe the northern air really is better for you.

When the lights came on, I sat for a while and got my bearings. Then I got up and saw Paul at the door. He must have seen the play, too. He came over and asked me how I had liked it. For a minute, I thought I might not talk to him because he smokes, and I don't like people who smoke, but after a little while I decided to answer.

"It was a bit overwhelming," I said. "But even so, I would have to say that it is the best play I have ever seen."

"Do you know what it was about?" he asked.

"No," I said. "But I'm working on it."

"Wisely put," he said, and he smiled. I saw that he was drinking a beer. My dad likes beer. I looked around and they were selling things to eat and tickets for drinks at the bar. I was still full from the french fries, but I liked the look of the ticket system so I bought one and traded it in for a glass of wine.

"Do you have any ID?" the bartender asked. I showed him my student card and he handed me the glass. I took a sip. Some wines are sort of snappy in your mouth, but this one wasn't. It tasted like fish. I left my glass, still full, on the corner of the bar and went back to talk to Paul.

"Where is June?" I asked. "Did she like the play?"

"June didn't come," Paul said. "She doesn't like to go out much."

"But it's dark," I said. "You'd think she wouldn't mind being at a play because you're in the dark most of the time."

"Especially with Pinter," said Paul, and I don't know what he meant by that.

"Because you said she comes out at night," I said. "She doesn't mind coming out in the dark."

"Sometimes it's not dark enough," Paul said, and then he put one hand up to his forehead. I thought he might be sad. This is one of the first times I have taken a good look at his face. He really does look like Indiana Jones. Then he went on talking. "Do you want to go for a walk? It's still early," he said.

I thought for a moment.

"No," I said. "I don't. There's been too many changes of plans already today." I thought of Kody. "Plus, I might be getting sick."

"See you tomorrow, maybe," he said. He sighed, and I wondered what that meant. In school I studied books about people's expressions and how you can tell someone's feelings from their mouths and eyebrows, but I don't remember Shauna talking to me at all about sighing. I never sigh, myself. Come to think of it, neither does she.

"See you," I answered. I sighed, just to see how it felt. It didn't feel like anything. I went outside and back to the restaurant. Mom's shift was done, and she came up to my room with me.

"Did you see Kody tonight?" she asked.

"No," I said. "He probably didn't see me, either. I was at a play."

"I missed you," she said.

"I phoned," I reminded her.

"I know. It just seems like you and I aren't spending much time together. What did you do tonight?"

"I went to a play. I told you on the phone." I sighed.

"I know, I mean, tell me about it."

"I forget what it was called. And I forget who the author was. And I don't know what it was about, really. But it was interesting. People repeated what each other said, and sometimes said the opposite of what somebody else said. They also seemed like they were afraid of what was going to happen next. And there were these long pauses in between what people said to each other. One character couldn't sleep." Then I sighed again.

"Are you feeling tired, or what's all that sighing about?" Mom asked.

"The play was good," I went on. "It's part of a festival, all plays by the same—"

"Sounds interesting," Mom interrupted. There she goes again. Why does she !!&%$%@@@ do this? She says something sounds interesting when she really means she doesn't want to hear about it anymore. What's the use in saying the opposite of what you really mean? It's just like lying.

"Do you mind if Danny and I go out tomorrow night?" she asked. "We thought that, because it's Friday night, we'd go out on a date. Will you be okay?"

"Sure. I'll be fine," I said. "Why do you want to go out with him?"

"Do you mean tomorrow or anytime?"

"Both."

"Well, he treats me nice. He has a great sense of humor."

Mom rubbed my hands the way I like, thumbs against the insides of my palms.

"You could come, too, if you like. On the date."

"No, I'm better here," I said. "I'm eighteen and a half. You don't have to take me everywhere."

Tomorrow I'm counting on getting Shauna's postcard.

Friday July 5
How Kody Already Became Someone Else's Boyfriend

Today so far has been a !!&%$%@@@ day. I am in my room because today I ran into Kody and he acted like he didn't know me. At least, he acted like he didn't want to talk to me. I was in the nature center, using one of the discovery programs on a computer, and he was coming in with the girl who takes over from Rose, the person who works in the book section in the morning. Rose and the afternoon girl usually switch places at noon. Kody and the afternoon girl were laughing and he didn't see me at first and he was eating sunflower seeds and spitting them back onto the front step. Then he looked over toward me and said, "Uh-oh. Here's trouble."

I looked around, but I didn't see anything wrong.

"Hi," I said.

"Hi," he said, but he kind of mumbled, and then he put the sunflower seeds in his pocket.

After the afternoon girl took Rose's place, he went over to the desk and pretended to buy books from her. She kept saying, "Don't be silly. You don't want to learn about conifers," and,

"Kody, I never knew you were so interested in squirrels." The girl has a ring that goes right through the side of her nose. If she blows her nose, I bet she'll rip it right out. I hope she does.

Paul was busy directing some kids in a scavenger hunt, and their parents were standing around waiting for them to be done. Julie asked me if I was coming back in the afternoon to see the film on wolves.

"No," I said loudly, trying not to look at the blister on her arm, but looking at it anyway. "I have better things to do than hang around here."

I meant that I had better things to do than hang around Kody and that girl, but I think I hurt Julie's feelings because she said, "Suit yourself," and when I brushed past Paul, he asked if everything was okay. Usually people ask if things are okay when they can tell they're not okay.

"Nope, things are stupid," I said, even louder, and then I couldn't help it—I just went off on a rant. My IQ went down at least forty points. First I yelled that the building was too hot, and then I asked why there were so many people all crowded in— couldn't they see that there wasn't room for all of them—and then I said a bunch of other loud things that I can't remember. I didn't swear, though. I remembered that there were little kids present, and I erased the swearing before it came out of my mouth. Paul took me by the elbow and led me outside. Then he looked like he didn't know what to say to me.

"I'm just going to take some deep breaths!" I said. Paul lit a cigarette.

"Do you mind?" I said. "I'm trying to take some deep breaths and you're lighting a !!&%$%@@@ cigarette!"

"Hey, don't get your shirt in a knot," he said. "There's more than one way to calm down."

"You're picking a !!&%$%@@@ way to calm down," I said. "And my shirt is not in a knot. In fact, I'm wearing a dress."

"Okay, okay," he said. "What made you so mad, anyway?"

"I don't want to talk about it." Then I started talking about it. I told him that Kody had almost been my boyfriend, but now he wanted to be that other girl's boyfriend, and it made me mad.

"So you really like him?" Paul asked.

"No. He is a person without much intuition. But he looks good in jeans."

Paul laughed.

"Come back in when you're feeling like it," he said. "And try not to blow the roof off next time."

I don't know what he meant by that last part. Well, maybe I do. Maybe I was yelling so hard he thought the roof was going to fly off. But that couldn't really happen.

I couldn't go back into the nature center because Kody was still in there, and anyway, I still felt too mad. I came to my room and for some reason, I took a big felt marker I found on the stairs and put a big X on the outside of my door. Now I've just slammed the door and I'm lying on my bed typing this journal, which isn't very much help at all. The breath feels squeezed right out of me.

That person, I can't remember who it was right now, who said the pen was mightier than the sword—I think they were wrong. I think the eraser is actually the most powerful tool. I wish there was an eraser that could erase the things a person did. And erase other people. Writing things down doesn't erase anything. What's done is done, and that really sucks.

I am Healthy, But What Good is It?

I am not writing another entry today because everybody's !!&%$%@@@ stupid and my mom is mad at me for mouthing off at Danny and it's not my fault for mouthing off because she ordered something I didn't want to eat at supper and told me I had to eat it. I told her I didn't want to, and then Danny got involved.

"As long as you're in my restaurant, you'll eat," he said.

"See!" I said to Mom. "Nine!" Then I told Danny that the last thing I'd be doing is eating anymore at his restaurant and that his customers probably all got sick from the bad food and then when Mom and Danny followed me upstairs they found out what I'd done to my door. I don't remember what I said and did after that, but I know it was bad.

I did not get a postcard from Shauna. She is not my friend.

The only good thing is that I did not get sick from the germs. I am still completely healthy.

Saturday July 6
Bimbo and Danny Both Have Five Letters

Mom said I had to apologize to Danny for what I said yesterday about him being a male bimbo. I called him that when he gave me the orders to clean off my door. She also said I have to apologize to both of them for making them miss their date last night because they couldn't leave when I was having a meltdown.

I tried to tell her that it wasn't my fault I had the meltdown, but she wouldn't listen. I eventually did say sorry, but I didn't mean it. Then I cleaned my door with the T-shirt I'd won at the clean water booth. Then she took me shopping and bought me a bathing suit. I put it in the closet, but I know I'm not going to wear it.

Mom and Danny have gone swimming. It's a nice day and they said they weren't going to waste it hanging around here with me and if I was going to be a sourpuss I could just stay in alone. Fine. I will stay here until this afternoon and maybe longer. I will go out after supper, however, because this is the night that Paul and the other people he works with are putting on a show at the outdoor theater.

Although I looked for him when we were downtown, I did not see Kody today. This is good because I do not want to see him. It is also bad because my IQ is back to normal, and I might interpret things differently about him and that afternoon girl. Like, what if she is his sister?

Orchids and Boyfriends Both Disappear Easily

It's still Saturday, but as I write this it is going to change into Sunday as it is almost midnight. I was up late because Danny and Mom took me to the outdoor theater, and the show didn't end until eleven and then we came back and had hot chocolate. The show was about bears. Paul and two other naturalists talked and showed slides, and then there was a short film and a singsong with a guitar, which Julie played.

Waskesiu is home to many black bears, and we don't usually see grizzlies here because they mostly live in the mountains, like in British Columbia. The bears are smart and try not to be close to people unless they have been trained to hang around by people who leave out food or garbage.

After the show, I began to think a lot about the bears, and, although it was dark, I tried to see into the woods around the parking lot, just in case one was in there, watching. The bears are bigger than I thought they'd be, and they can hurt humans. If a black bear attacks you, you're not supposed to lie down and play dead like you would if it were a grizzly. You're supposed to make lots of loud noise and try to get away. Even if you climb a tree, that's not going to save you because black bears can climb. I can't climb trees very well, so I probably wouldn't have tried this method of escape.

As we walked into the parking lot, I saw a boy and a girl sitting on one of the benches under a streetlamp. They were kissing. I got a good look. The afternoon girl is not his sister.

In the car on the way back, Mom kept saying what a nice time that was and asking me if I had enjoyed it. I dug my fingernails into my palms. Then she asked me what I thought about staying in Waskesiu now that we'd been here a week and if I missed my friends or my things back home.

I don't really have any friends. I used to when I was a little kid; at least, I remember getting invited to birthday parties and things. I liked going to parties until I got there, and then I wanted to go home. The invitations stopped when I was in grade six or seven. Then I would go to a movie with someone once in a while, but it was usually Mom that did the planning.

"I miss my music," I said. "And I miss Hammy," I added before remembering that Mom has told me not to talk about gerbils.

"That's different," Danny said. "He's dead, isn't he? You can't miss something dead in the same way you miss things you've just left behind because it's not the same."

"It is the same," I said and then muttered under my breath, "Seventeen words—that's a record." I looked straight at Danny: "It's just the !!&%$%@@@ same." But Mom told me not to talk back, so I stopped talking altogether and just listened to them. I am thinking about this again now, and I'm sure I'm right. When you are missing something you've left behind, it could be dead or lost so that you never find it again. You never really know, when you don't have something, what its condition is. That's why you grieve about it to the same degree—because you just don't know.

I kept trying to fill my mind with other things. I saw a poster on a bulletin board at the outdoor theater that said the play I saw before—*The Birthday Party*—is going to be on again tomorrow afternoon. I thought about how I want to go and see it. Maybe I'll understand it better if I see it a second time.

I went to show Mom the yellow lady's slipper near where we had parked, and it was gone. I knew exactly where to look for it, but the flower wasn't there. The leaves were there, though, and the stalk, sort of dried up, transparent under the light. Three little brown triangles hung down where the flower had been. The sepals.

Mom didn't want to talk about the lady's slipper. She kept asking me about Kody. Like where was he staying, and was I going to see him again? Finally, I told her that I wouldn't be seeing him again because he was dead.

"Taylor, stop making up stories," she said, and she had that H in her forehead.

"Well, he's dead to me," I said, and I think she got the message because she stopped asking.

Now I'm chewing gum and sitting on my bed, and I can hear the waves lapping at the shore along with the sound of my clock ticking. I wonder if Shauna can hear waves where she is. At first I didn't like it, but now it's getting to be okay. It's a nice background for listening to Mom and Danny fighting. I've tried to hear if they're fighting about me, but I just can't tell.

Monday July 8
Is the Number 846 Possible or Necessary or Both?

I feel badly that I didn't write yesterday, but too much was happening and I forgot. I'm sorry I didn't write. I know I said I'd write every day, but I guess it's okay if I missed just once.

Yesterday afternoon I went to see *The Birthday Party* again. It was on during a matinee. I did understand it better this time. It's a play about this guy called Stanley who's afraid of things that other people don't expect him to be afraid of. He stays in his room at a boardinghouse, and the lady who runs it has to force him to come down for breakfast. He doesn't like the cornflakes and says so, and everybody's surprised. I understand why he wouldn't like them, though. Cornflakes are hard and crunchy, and they feel dangerous in your mouth.

Stanley can't sleep. That's why he's so obnoxious and says things that make Meg angry. He tells her that the house is a mess. It's just because everything jars him: the lights, the clutter. I can understand that, too.

As I watched the play, I started thinking that maybe Stanley is a lot like me. He wants to go off on his own, but he can't function without Meg. She looks after him like a parent. He wants to go and get a job, but he can't because he's afraid. Stanley's afraid of lots of things. Like in the play he was afraid of a van coming. He can't predict who would be in it. Most people would say, "Don't be silly, it's just a van, and some people are coming in it." It's useless when people tell you not to worry, though—there's plenty to worry about in this world.

I started thinking that maybe the secret is that you can worry all you like, but you just have to go ahead without letting on that you're afraid. That's what I want to tell Stanley. Just to go on.

When I came out of the theater, I was surprised to see that it was still light. I somehow thought it was already night, that the day had passed completely while I was at the play. I stood and listened for a minute to the other people as they came out. One person said, "Pinter is the master of the pause, isn't he?" And another person said, "Yes, the Pinter pause is a very clever device." I felt smart to have noticed the pauses, myself.

One line from the play keeps coming back to me. "Is the number 846 possible or necessary?" Goldberg says this when they are both interrogating Stanley. First Stanley says, "Neither," and then he says, "Both." I wonder what the right answer is. I can see how Stanley would say, "Neither," because when you're in a bad spot, nothing is possible or necessary. I can also see how he would say it is possible and necessary because as soon as a number is possible, it's necessary. Like, it's important in the whole scheme of numbers. If you are aware of it, you can't do without it. How could you count to ten without mentioning seven? I do not see how Goldberg's answer, that it is necessary, but not possible, could be right. I wonder what Paul thinks.

Having a boyfriend is both possible and necessary. It is possible because there are boys out there. It is necessary because once it's possible, a person needs to grow up and conduct themselves with adult behavior. I suppose it could be necessary without being possible, but this would be extremely discouraging.

I took a walk up to the golf course and saw three white-tailed deer grazing at the edge of the woods. I don't think they bite, but I wonder if they do. They look very fragile. All the time I was walking I thought about boyfriends, their necessity and their possibilities. Then I walked back to the restaurant and had supper with Mom. She was getting ready for an evening shift, and she said she liked these shifts best because she makes the most tips. I asked her about the deer and she said not to be silly. I wasn't being silly; I just wanted to know.

I went up and down the beach a particular number of times and then strolled around the townsite toward home. It isn't really home, but I call it that because it's more comforting. I went across the road and up the steps of the nature center, to see if there were any notices about tomorrow. A poster said there was going to be a nature walk along the lake at 10:00 A.M.

I walked out to the pier, and when I was coming back, I saw Paul standing on the beach, looking out at the sunset. He was standing beside a wheelchair. His wife, June, was in the wheelchair. I started to walk over to them, but decided to take another route. Then Paul called my name.

"Taylor!" he called. "Come on over here."

I went over to them. His wife has very long, straight, blonde hair. She looks like Gwyneth Paltrow, who played Emma in the movie with the same name. We saw the movie last year because we studied Jane Austen. Mrs. Thomson always asked us to make personal connections to what we were reading or seeing, and after I saw the movie, I said that Emma was lucky because she had a lot of friends. I'm not very successful with friends. In fact, now that Shauna isn't my friend, I don't have any friends.

I wrote an essay about friendship once. I said it was the only kind of ship that could go in more than one direction at the same time. I copied that statement off the Internet. At the time, I didn't really understand what it meant. Now I think I do understand. The direction I'm going is that I want Shauna to be my friend. The direction she's going is just the opposite. Our friendship is pulling us apart.

"I had a gerbil named June," I said to June. "I quite enjoy gerbils. They are smart enough to be interesting, but not smart enough to use tools or try to escape their cages. Sometimes, they escape their cages by accident, and then you have to chase them. Once, June got under the kitchen sink, and it was very difficult to get her out. We used bribery with peanut butter and then slapped a margarine container on top of her. She was the best eater of all my gerbils, and she particularly liked radishes."

"Oh," said June. I wondered if maybe I should ask her a question. It's difficult trying to see inside people's heads, but that's what you're supposed to do if you're having a conversation with them. I much prefer looking at their hands. June's hands are slim and white, and you can see the blue veins along their tops.

"You could have a gerbil, except for your cat," I said.

"What?" she said.

"Your cat would eat it," I said.

"Oh," she said, and she brushed her hair back from her face.

"Does your cat act like it has autism?" I asked. "On Tony Attwood's website there is an article that says cats are autistic dogs."

"Uh, I don't really know," said June. "She likes to sit on the television."

I looked at her hair for a few minutes. It was really smooth.

"Is it dark enough?" I asked her.

"What?" she said.

"Paul said you only liked coming out when it was dark, and I think maybe it's not dark enough yet. It will get darker, though, very soon."

June made a funny sound in her throat. Paul said, "It's just fine. It doesn't have to be dark—we just like coming out in the dark, that's all."

"I saw *The Birthday Party* again this afternoon," I said. "I understood it better this time. Stanley might have Asperger's Syndrome, and this is something I can relate to."

"What?" said June.

"Asperger's Syndrome," I said. "It's a kind of autism that people get if parts of their brains are too small and other parts are extra large. I have it. The amygdala, which is part of the brain, is smaller than in most people's brains. You get born with Asperger's Syndrome if there's the right balance of heredity and environment."

"Like orchids," said Paul, softly.

When June didn't say anything, I put some gum in my mouth and then said, "Stanley is sure afraid of a lot of things. Like, he was afraid of that new person coming. Then he made up the story about a van coming with a wheelbarrow in it—to him this was very scary. That reminded me of when I was little and my dad bought a new lawnmower and the people came in a van to deliver it. I heard my parents talking about the delivery, and when I heard that a man was coming in a van to bring the lawnmower, I went and hid. I kept thinking of how awful it would be to open the back of the van, expecting to see seats and see a lawnmower instead."

Nobody said anything. I thought of the deer I had seen.

"Deer don't bite," I said.

"It was nice meeting you," said June. She looked up at Paul and said, "It's time we were getting along."

"Aren't you getting along?" I asked. "That happened to my parents and they got a divorce. But there's counseling. If people go to counseling, it can help."

Paul took out a cigarette. I think he uses cigarettes the same way I use gum. I have decided that just because he smokes, he might not be a bad person. He just has a bad habit, although it could be considered a good habit if it keeps him from doing worser things like melting down, the way I do if I'm stressed and don't have gum.

"I meant getting along home," said June. "It's time we were getting back."

"Have you seen *The Birthday Party*?" I asked her. "It's very good. It's at the hall. Sometimes you can understand it, and sometimes you can't, but it's very interesting, nevertheless. I mean that, too. I would never say it was interesting if it wasn't, not like some people."

I didn't mean to be rude. I wasn't trying to insinuate that June was one of those people, although she does remind me of my mom.

"I like your hair," I said, to try and say something positive. "In the sun, it would look like fiber-optic cables."

"Thank you," said June.

Paul pushed June's wheelchair off the sand onto the sidewalk, and I walked beside them up the hill. I don't blame June for not liking the light. I can understand that. Some people find darkness softer on their skin. I am one of those people. That's another reason I don't like swimming—because water weighs on you the same way light does. Sometimes, you have to get used to it, though, for bathing and things. Sometimes, you just have to. I wanted to say that to June, but I didn't have the courage.

Tuesday July 9
If Stanley were Here, He Would Understand Me

I didn't write down everything yesterday. I said
I'd write down things here so that I could
understand them better, but I didn't write
down the main thing about the play. I can
write it now, though, because I'm calmer and
drinking water from my water bottle and
chewing on the straw. The play brought back
some memories that aren't happy ones, and at first,
I didn't like that, but after a while, it actually feels
good to think that Stanley would understand what
I have been through.

I liked it that Stanley didn't want to have a birthday party,
and that when his landlady tried to give him one, he attempted
to go out. Then, when those two bad guys, McCann and
Goldberg, came to his party and planned to stay at the boardinghouse, he told them there wasn't any room.

When I was a kid, I didn't like birthday parties either.
Birthday parties would have been great if there were no other
people there. I was always afraid that maybe the kids we'd invited
would want to stay. What if they did? What if we had a party and

the kids got used to using our stuff and just decided to stay? It was bad enough for a short time, having all the noise in the house and the clutter and the differences from usual, but what if it was going to go on *forever*?

It was my eighth birthday, and I was hiding under the bed and my dad wanted me to come out and be polite to my friends and my mom said, "Just leave her there; she's not feeling well," but Dad grabbed me by the shoes and pulled me out and dragged me downstairs. I was screaming and crying and one of the other girls said, "Here comes the Freaker!" and I heard it. That's what the kids had started calling me at school when I had a meltdown. *The Freaker.*

My dad was always saying that Mom spoiled me and let me do whatever I wanted and Mom was always saying that he didn't understand me and that he should try harder. But he wasn't around long enough to try harder. After my eighth birthday, he and Mom had a big fight and then later Mom threw a lot of his things out of the upstairs window.

I had nightmares about that for years because I was outside in the garage when she was throwing the things out the window. I was in the garage because, sometimes, when I was upset, I would go out and count the spare tires. We had a lot of spare tires leaning up against the inside wall of the garage. I would use the chain to open the big door and let in the light, and then I'd count the tires. It was very comforting. We always had three groups of seven.

When I was in the garage on my birthday, I saw his things flying down into the snow, and at first I thought that maybe she was going to throw Dad out the window, too, and I didn't want to watch, but how could you not watch if your dad was being thrown out the upstairs window? It took me awhile to realize that the Volvo was gone, and so Dad must be in it. I don't know what happened to his things, if he came back to pick them up or what. The next day they just weren't in the driveway anymore. Eventually, I learned that he was in Cody, Wyoming. And the Volvo was with him.

The postmark on the letters he sends says Cody, Wyoming. That's the only thing I read from the letters. I never actually open any of the envelopes. It's easier not to open them because I don't know what they are going to say. I just put them somewhere and eventually throw them out. I got a letter from my father today, and I put it in the other sandal, the one that isn't holding the social story Mom wrote about going to the movies.

I've had a feeling since this last Christmas, when I came home early, that I won't be going back anytime soon. Maybe never. Mom says that I should write my father, but I don't feel like it. I wouldn't know what to say. She doesn't try to make me, so I think she understands. I'm glad because that means she must have forgiven me for making my dad leave. She says it wasn't easy for her when he left. She had to get a job and, before she could do that, she had to go to secretarial school and we ate a lot of macaroni and cheese, which is okay because I like macaroni and cheese, except I eat it without the cheese because then it's white and I like it better.

The other thing that happened was that at the end of the play, when McCann and Goldberg are yelling at Stanley, I got so angry at them that I almost stood up and yelled, too. They weren't fighting fair. They kept asking him questions and then interrupting before he had a chance to answer. Sometimes, people used to talk to me like that. Kids at school. So I understand how Stanley felt.

I remember this one time when everybody was gathered around me on the playground. I don't know where the teacher was. Maybe there wasn't one out there; maybe she forgot she was on supervision. And the kids were yelling, "Lion King, Lion King!" That's what people were calling me because I had a Lion King lunch kit. I guess I must have been in about fourth grade, and maybe nobody by that time carried lunch kits with cartoons on them, but I had always used it and I liked it. Anyway, when they started calling me that, I thought they had changed my name to Lion King and I couldn't stand it. You change the name of something, and then maybe everything changes. Maybe nobody would recognize me anymore, and I'd go home and my mom wouldn't even know me.

Every time they called me that name, I'd go crazy. I felt completely powerless. There was nothing I could do to make them stop. Now I know that because I went crazy, it made them want to do it more. Shauna says that some people are like that— if they can get a rise out of you, it makes them happy. So on this one day, kids were gathered around me and yelling and it was almost like I had blacked out, except I know that I was running around and trying to kick and hit kids. I know that I did more than just *try* because later I had to write apology notes for hurting kids and a copy was sent home to their parents.

A teacher finally came out and stopped us. This is a good thing because I don't know what I would have done if nobody had come. The thing is, when I think about it, it seems to go on forever and I can't make it stop. In my memory, the teacher separating us is like the exclamation point at the end of the paragraph. She made it stop, and if she hadn't done that, I still see myself kicking and hitting. I got expelled for three days. That's when Mom took me to the doctor, and I think she found out my diagnosis around that time. I went to a number of different doctors that year. When I went back to the school, the teachers made me and the other kids play together. That was so much like in *The Birthday Party*, when Stanley had to play Blind Man's Bluff with the others. I could tell that he was miserable and wished he weren't playing, and that's why he started giggling later because it was the only alternative to crying.

Fear, Swimming and Bears

I wrote that other stuff in the morning, and now it is night. I should tell about what happened today. When I got to the nature center at ten, nobody else had come for the trail walk, so Julie decided to stay and sort through slides for a picture show they are going to be doing next Friday night at the outdoor theater. She had on long sleeves, so I wasn't tempted to look at her arm with the mark on it. Paul said he'd do the walk with me if I still wanted to. I said I did, and off we went.

The trail starts on the bank near the nature center, so we didn't have to drive anywhere. We had walked along for a little while when Paul said, "Sorry that my wife wasn't too friendly on Sunday."

"That's okay," I said. "She's probably missing walking too much to think about anything else."

"Could be," he said.

"I know that I would really miss walking if I couldn't do it anymore," I said. "I might be afraid of things that could happen to me if I couldn't walk, too. Like if I fell out of my wheelchair and nobody was there to pick me up."

Paul didn't say anything.

"A person has to try and be brave," I said. "If you are in the woods and you see deer and you don't know if they bite, you can always ask someone."

"I think you are brave," said Paul.

"Thank you," I said.

"You're welcome," he said.

"I'm sleeping pretty good," I said. "It's easier to be brave when you've had enough sleep."

"That's good," he said.

It's funny, talking to Paul. I can have whole conversations with him and not once worry about making the right choices in terms of what I say. I can say anything to him, and he just listens and answers back.

We walked for a while more, and then Paul said, "Taylor, what you said before about Stanley in the play being afraid of the unknown was very true. Fear is a powerful emotion, isn't it?"

I nodded.

"I don't know how to help her," he said, and his voice was kind of shaky. "She's afraid, I guess, all the time. And I can't stop it."

"Nobody can stop it for her," I said. "You have to face your own fear because nobody else can really see it clearly. This is because everybody has a different perspective."

"But how do you stop being afraid?" he asked, and his hands made little jerks up and down.

"I guess you don't really ever stop," I said, after thinking about it for a few minutes. "But you just have to go on. Like Stanley. You just have to get up in the morning and see what happens. Even though it's hard."

"Sometimes, I think June doesn't want to get up in the morning," Paul said, brushing down spiderwebs from the trail ahead. "Sometimes, I think she's completely given up."

"Giving up is bad," I said.

"I think that's what happened to my father. He just gave up," said Paul. Then he said, "I probably shouldn't be telling you all this. You don't need to hear about all my baggage."

I wasn't sure what he meant by that. I know baggage is suitcases.

"Sometimes, it's okay to let someone else carry your suitcase," I said. "But only if their hands are clean."

Paul laughed a lot when I said that. I'm glad I made him feel better.

"Is the number 846 possible or necessary?" I asked.

"Both," said Paul, grinning. "But I've been in spaces when I would have said neither."

"So have I," I said.

After a few minutes I pointed down beside the path. "I saw that flower in one of the books. It's called blue-eyed grass. I like it. It's the same color as my bedroom back home."

"It's the same color as your eyes," said Paul.

"Who found him?" I asked.

There was a little silence.

"Oh," said Paul. "My sister. She was going downstairs to look for some Lego because I was making her a car."

"How did he do it?"

"He used the rope from the clothesline."

"And just pulled it tight?"

"Pulled it tight while he was standing on a chair and then kicked the chair away."

"While the rope was tied to something else?"

"Yup."

"It wouldn't have taken very long."

"No. Not long enough for anybody to do anything."

"What did your sister do?"

"Came and got me. He was looking after us while our mother was at work."

"What did you do?"

"It's funny, really. First I put the chair back under his feet because that looked better. Then I called my grandma, and she called 911."

"But he was already dead."

"As a doornail."

Dead as a doornail. I have heard that phrase before, and it doesn't make any sense. If you're dead, you're dead. You can't be more or less dead, can you? And why would a doornail be a good comparison? And what is a doornail?

"He was probably taking medication," I said. "I was on medication once, and I wanted to die."

"I think maybe he should have been on medication," said Paul. "But we didn't know any better. We thought he was just grumpy when he was depressed as hell." He lit a cigarette, but I didn't say anything about it.

"I wish I had something . . ." he said, finally, "something to let me know he really did care about me, even though he stopped caring about himself. A letter, maybe. Yeah, that's what I'd like. Just a letter."

"But if you had a letter from your father, and it was sealed and put away, you wouldn't really open it?" I asked. Paul took a deep breath before he answered.

"You bet," he said quietly. "You bet I would."

We walked along on the path beside the lake for a few minutes, and then a boat came in about ten meters from shore and the driver yelled, "Look out up ahead. Bears on the trail." Before I could react to this, I saw a bear just up ahead of us and then another.

"Cubs," said Paul, and he took a step backward. I took a step back, too, and I saw another little bear join the others. Three cubs. I remembered what it had said in the film, that mother bears are generally only dangerous if you are a threat to their young. I turned and ran into the water toward the boat. Even though I don't like water, I threw myself in and began flailing my arms and legs because I know swimming is faster than walking. When I got to the side of the boat, the man reached over and pulled me in.

I sat dripping on the seat, and the man and a lady looked at me.

"Good thing it's a hot day," she said. "Are you afraid of bears?" I nodded.

"Is it okay that I am in your boat?" I asked.

"Well, sure," the man said.

"It won't sink because of weight restrictions?" I asked.

"No, we're fine," said the woman, laughing and handing me her coat. I wiped my face on it. I don't know why she was laughing.

"Where would you like me to take you?" asked the man. I looked back toward the shore. Paul was walking back along the water, away from the cubs. He wasn't walking slowly, but he wasn't running, either.

"Follow that guy," I said. The woman laughed even harder.

Paul looked at me and pointed out to the pier. I said to the man, "Please take me to the pier." I'm glad I remembered my manners. The man drove the boat over to the pier, and I climbed out. It was a hot day, but I was shivering even though I had the coat on.

The woman said, "I'll need my coat back, now," and so I had to give it back.

When Paul came up to me, I could see that he was laughing, too.

"Why are you laughing?" I asked. All the laughing was making me !!&%$%@@@ furious.

"You look very wet," he said.

"You'd be wet, too, if you'd jumped in the lake!" I yelled.

"I thought you didn't like swimming," he chuckled.

"People can change their minds!" I yelled even louder and he stopped laughing.

"Don't get your shirt in a knot," he said.

This really !!&%$%@@@ me off. I wasn't even wearing a shirt because I had on my jean dress.

"That's just like you!" I screamed. "You say stupid things that nobody can figure out!"

"Hold on," he said.

"There you go again! What should I hold onto! You're talking nuts. And I thought the mother bear was going to come and kill me and now I'm all wet and I hate being wet. I hate it so much! And the water was really cold! And all sorts of animals and fish and other people have been in that water, which makes it really disgusting!"

"You're right to be mad at me. I shouldn't have laughed," he said.

"You're right!" I was still yelling, but I took a deep breath and protected what was left of my IQ. My dress was starting to get dry in the sun, and I realized I wasn't sick or anything from all the fish germs. I reached into my pocket and took out some gum. The package was wet with lake water, and I deliberated. Then I took a deep breath and put a piece in my mouth. It was spearmint.

"I don't know why I went in the water," I said, taking off my wet shoes. I was thinking that I had done something stupid, which was why everybody was laughing at me. If there's one thing I hate more than being wet with lake water, it's being stupid.

"It's your survival instinct," said Paul. "Nothing wrong with that. The mother wasn't very far behind the cubs. Good thing she was more interested in the berries than in chasing us."

"Were they bearberries?" I said. I meant this as a joke.

"Wild strawberries," he said.

"I'm hungry," I said.

"How about ice cream?" asked Paul. So that is why we walked up the hill to the little store and Paul bought me a vanilla ice cream cone and I sat in the sun and ate it. I always pick vanilla because it's white and I like eating white things. The worst kind

I could pick is rum 'n' raisin because it's yellow. That's the kind Paul picked, but I tried not to watch him eat it.

We went back to the nature center, and Julie was sorting photographs. She asked me why I was carrying my shoes, and I told her what had happened. I said I would rather have bare feet than go home and get my sandals, and she said she liked bare feet best, too.

"When did your house burn down?" I asked her.

"What?" she said.

"Your house. When did it burn down and catch you in the fire and burn your arm?" I asked.

She shook her head.

"My house didn't burn down. I just pulled a pot of water off the stove when my kookum was over making soup. I was only five. That's how I got this scar."

"Did it hurt?" I asked.

"Yeah, but I sure learned not to go near the stove again. Still hate cooking today!"

"I am not an enthusiast, either," I said.

It was almost time for the afternoon girl to come, and I didn't want to take a chance on Kody walking her to work because I don't want to see him again. I went back to the restaurant, but I wasn't hungry because of the ice cream, so I just had some french fries. Mom was still working, but she said she was glad to see me and to wait around for her to be done and we could go for a walk together. Then she noticed I was a little damp and she asked why and I said, "I jumped in the lake," and she got the H in her forehead and said why hadn't I put on the new bathing suit she'd gotten me and I said it is a long story and I would tell her later.

Friday July 12
I Am Working in the Bookstore!

Now I've missed writing for two whole days. I'm really sorry about that because I know I planned to write every day. But a lot has happened and I haven't had very much time to write. On Wednesday when I went to the nature center, Paul was taking books out of boxes. "It's not really my job," he said when I came in, "But Mandy, the girl who works the bookstore in the afternoons, quit yesterday and didn't even finish her shift. All this new stock came in, and it's got to go somewhere. Nell Thomson, the owner, is on her way, but I'm not sure who she'll be able to hire on short notice."

"I could help you," I said. "I am very good at taking things out of boxes. I'm very good at putting things back in boxes, as well."

"Okay, that'd be great," he said. "Rose is busy counting the cash from yesterday, and I've got my own stuff to take care of."

"My English teacher is named Mrs. Thomson," I said. "But it's probably not the same one, right?"

"Probably not," said Paul. "This Mrs. Thomson lives up here full time. Rich as a skunk. Lives in one of the big cabins along the lakefront."

"I have a lot of boxes in my room back home," I said, taking a bunch of books out of the nearest box. "I have fifteen boxes, and I've sorted the stuff in my room to go into each box. Like, all my shirts are in a box. All my socks are in a box. I have boxes for everything."

"Why did you do that?" asked Paul.

"I like the idea of things being in order, and putting things away in boxes just makes good sense."

"Is that part of having Asperger's Syndrome?" asked Paul.

"I'm not sure," I said. "It could just be part of being related to my mother. She likes things in order, too." He laughed.

We worked in silence for a few minutes. Rose finished counting the money and came to help.

"About one in 250 people are born with Asperger's Syndrome," I said.

"I've heard of it before," said Rose. "I have a cousin in California who has it."

"I bet he's a boy," I said.

"Yes, he is," said Rose.

"Most people with autism are boys," I said. "In fact, I have only ever met one other girl with Asperger's Syndrome, at a social club I went to one summer. She was weird."

"Why was she weird?" asked Paul.

"She kept putting her hands up in front of her eyes. It made her look mentally challenged," I said.

When no one said anything, I went on.

"Could be the light was bothering her, like it bothers me. But you don't see me putting my hands up in front of my eyes. That's how people start picking on you, when you do weird things like that."

"People say Einstein and Michelangelo both had Asperger's Syndrome," said Rose.

"Really," said Paul.

"My mother read about it because of my cousin," said Rose. She talked about her cousin for a while, but I don't remember what else she said because I wasn't interested. There are twenty million people in the world with Asperger's Syndrome, and why would I want to know about them all? It would be like learning about every person in Australia.

After we unpacked the boxes, the bookstore Mrs. Thomson came in, and she talked about what they were going to do about the afternoon. Rose said she couldn't work all day because she had other plans for later.

"The wind's come up, finally," Mrs. Thomson said. "I planned to be out there windsurfing. Maybe we should just hang up a closed sign on the till. I hate to do that, though. Business is business. Couldn't you change your plans?" she asked Rose.

Paul looked at me.

"Maybe Taylor could help you out," he said. "Even just for a few days, until you advertise and hire someone long term."

I started to shake my head, but he kept talking.

"Taylor comes in here every day, and she really knows the place."

"Oh no," I said, taking out a piece of gum and putting it in my mouth.

"Rose could show you what to do this morning," Paul went on. "It would really help us out."

Mrs. Thomson nodded her head. She said, "If you're interested, that would be great. Anything to solve this problem fast. I've got the boat on the beach."

"Maybe she could work until the end of the week," Paul suggested. "And then you could see."

"Sounds good," said Mrs. Thomson. "All right, Taylor? It'll be minimum wage."

I put a second piece of gum in my mouth and chewed for three seconds.

"Okay," I said, looking at Paul and not breathing. "I'll do it."

After Mrs. Thomson left, I gasped and sat down with a stitch in my side.

"It'll be okay, Taylor," Paul said. "You'll do fine."

"Come on behind the counter," said Rose. "I'll show you how to work the cash register."

I stood up. My legs felt like blisters, all watery.

"I don't need an EMF Detector, do I?" I asked, remembering that Rose had one.

"I've got it in my pocket," Rose whispered. "But they don't like me to use it at work. I have tried it in here, but no luck."

"No luck?" I asked.

"No ghosts," she said.

This is how I learned what an EMF Detector does. I am glad I don't have to use it. I don't believe in ghosts.

I watched how she used the cash register. It wasn't hard.

"Do you mind having a name like Rose?" I asked her. "I mean, doesn't it get confusing having the same name as a flower?"

"No, I don't mind. I guess I'm used to it," she said. "And at least it has a nice sound to it. Not like wild bergamot or something."

"Bergamot—that would be a worse name," I agreed.

So that is how I got my first job! All this time, I've been worrying about the fall and having to get work or take classes, and making all these decisions has been weighing on me. But having a job isn't so hard. I am already pretty good at it.

When people come in, I say, "May I help you?" They usually say they're just looking, and then I let them walk around and look at stuff. I keep my eye on them, especially the young ones, to make sure they don't put anything into their pockets. When they've finished and start to leave, I say, "Thanks for dropping by." This is what Rose told me to say, and it was an easy script to memorize.

If people want to buy something, it's a little harder, but I know what to do. I punch in the amount listed on the back of the book or toy and then press Cash. The drawer at the bottom of the cash register pops open, and I do not stand close when it does this. Then I put their money in and count out the correct change. I am very good with money, so this isn't a problem at all. Then I push the drawer shut and say, "Thanks very much," and hand them their items in a bag.

I didn't know what to say to my mother about the job. First I asked her when her birthday was, and she made the H with her eyebrows.

"I'm thinking of buying you a present because at the moment I'm considering a job," I said, remembering the words Stanley had used in the play. "Now say the right thing back."

"What am I supposed to say?" she asked.

"You're supposed to say, 'You're not!'"

"You're not!" she said.

"I am. And it's a good job, too. In a bookstore."

"A bookstore," she said.

"Selling books," I said. "It is just for four days. But it might be for longer."

My mother said she was very impressed. She said she's going to come and see me at work on Saturday—and that's tomorrow—and maybe buy something. I don't know if I'll be working on Saturday, though. They might have hired someone else by then. I'm supposed to go to the nature center in the morning and talk to the boss. Julie told me to say that I have appreciated the opportunity to work in the bookstore and to let the boss know that I am available to continue if she needs me. It still freaks me out that her name is Mrs. Thomson. Just like my English teacher. I'm trying not to think about it. She does not look like my English teacher. My English teacher looks like Whoopie Goldberg.

After I told my mother about my job, I went to my sandal and took out the letter from my father. I tried to read a little of it through the envelope, but I couldn't make out any words. I tore a little corner off the envelope. Then I opened the whole thing.

It was a surprise. My father didn't congratulate me about having a job. I had predicted that he would—that's actually why I had the courage to open the letter in the first place. But now that I think about it, he wouldn't have known about my job. His perspective hasn't let him know about my job. The only way he'll know about my job is if someone builds bridges with words. Maybe that someone will have to be me.

In the letter he said that he had heard of something called an atomic watch. It uses computer chips to tell the time by collecting the exact information from an atomic clock in Boulder, Colorado. The clock picks up the time from a satellite. He said that this time was always correct.

He also said that he wants me to try coming out for a weekend in the fall. He said that maybe Christmas was too stressful because it was Christmas, and nobody does well at Christmas. He said that Thanksgiving would be good, if it was okay with me. He said he would wait and send money for the train ticket once I had made my decision.

I will have to think about it.

Even though it's in The Future, I will think about it anyway. I do not want to end up like Stanley, stuck in his room. Dormant.

Saturday July 13
Regular Hours

I get the job until the end of August! My hours will be one to five on weekdays, and one to six on Saturdays. Wow! I am so excited.

I am going to go look up the word paycheck in my dictionary. It is a word with which I have no experience.

The closest I can find in the dictionary is, "Check. An order or draft on a bank for money."

Wednesday July 17
At Last—A Plan

I am very sorry I haven't written, but I am a
working person now, and I don't have much
time for other things. I still get up at eight
o'clock and go for a walk, and then I go to the
nature center at ten. Sometimes I stay there,
and sometimes I go on the public trail walk
that they have planned. Julie always asks me
to name the plants for the people at the back of the
line because they can't always hear her if she is
guiding the walk from the front. I have learned to
walk at the back because I have an important job there.

I went to another Pinter play, but I can't remember the title.
The Pinter Festival ended on Sunday. I didn't like this play as much
as *The Birthday Party,* but it was still interesting. Paul came to the
play, too, and sat beside me. It was funny. At first we were sitting sort
of separately, but then our shoulders touched and I didn't mind.

Afterward, he bought me a Coke, which I shouldn't have had
because caffeine makes me feel a bit duplicated. I didn't want
wine again because of its tasting like fish. We went and sat on a
bench in the woods, overlooking the lake, and I was still feeling

my out-of-body experience. I told him all about a gerbil's digestion. The digestion of large quantities of vegetable matter requires a sizable stomach and long intestine; cellulose is a difficult thing to break down and digest. All herbivores have a sort of fermentation tank, where digestion is assisted by micro-organisms. This tank in rodents is called the caecum, and it's a pocket like a person's appendix.

When I got to the part about coprophagy, where rodents need to eat their own poop, he said that he thought that was disgusting, but that I explained it very well. It's essential for their well being, I said, because it helps digestion. Plus, the poop is rich in vitamin B1 and is kind of like a vitamin pill.

A squirrel came and chattered at us from one of the branches of a pine tree. I asked what kind of squirrel it was, and Paul said it was a red squirrel. I asked what it ate, and he said seeds of the pine and spruce. I asked if it bites, and Paul said it does not. It has the same tooth structure as a gerbil, I noted, because they're both rodents. They're part of the order Rodentia, which derives its name from the Latin word *rodere,* meaning "to gnaw." The interesting thing about their teeth is that they have a space between the incisors and the cheek teeth. The space is called a *diastema,* and it enables the animal to draw in the sides of its lips so it can gnaw without getting chips of material in its mouth.

"You should go into biology," Paul said. "You're very interested in plants and animals, and you remember a lot of facts about them."

"I don't know," I said. "I am afraid of going into anything."

"You could start with one class," he said. "The university allows that. Just start with one class for the first semester and then see."

"I don't know," I said, and all at once a picture of Stanley flashed across my mind. He was still in that room and he couldn't get out. I was not going to end up like that.

"Maybe I could," I said, and all at once I felt like smiling, so I did.

"I bet you could," said Paul.

"Have you ever taken a biology class?" I asked him.

"Yeah, lots of them," he said. "You'd find those classes easy."

So that is what makes me think that in the fall I will take one biology class. I might also try to find a job in a bookstore. I am very good at working in bookstores, and an employer in Saskatoon would be lucky to have me. Mrs. Thomson came in today to see how I was doing, and she said her bookstore was lucky to have me. I asked her if she knew my English teacher, whose name is also Mrs. Thomson and who looks like Whoopi Goldberg and she said she didn't. I wonder if Whoopi Goldberg has seen *The Birthday Party*. I wonder what she thinks about the character of Goldberg having the same name as her.

I also asked Mrs. Thomson if she knew any bookstore owners who needed any help in the fall, and she said that she just might. There is a big bookstore in Saskatoon and it hires a lot of people and she knows someone who works there. I told her that if I got a job there, then she'd know two people and she smiled and said that would be good.

It makes me feel relaxed to finally have a plan for the fall. First working here for the summer. Then working in a bookstore in the city and taking one biology class. I think I can handle that. I know I can.

Wednesday July 24
Another Orchid Moment

I have not written for a whole week. At first, I felt really bad when I forgot to write, but now, because nothing happened to me for not writing, I think it's okay. It's okay if you make a plan to write every day and then you only do it some of the time. A person has to be satisfied if that's the best you can do.

The summer is going really well. Our holiday is almost half over. I'm calling it a holiday, although it's not really a holiday because I'm working every afternoon except Sundays.

Today, I went on the Kingsmere nature trail with a group from the nature center, and I found a sparrow's egg lady's slipper. It was just off the trail, near the river. I was excited that I had found something very rare. I showed the others, and one of the kids who came with their parents was going to pick it, but Julie gave a big lecture about how we never pick flowers in a national park.

The bottom petal was curled up into a puffy white shoe, and it looked clean and fresh. Inside the shoe it was yellow and dotted with reddish spots. I thought it was a white lady's slipper, but Paul said no, it wasn't. The white one would be whiter, with purple veins inside. It gave me a good feeling, seeing the orchid and knowing that this is not a common experience. Its Latin name is *Cypripedium passerinum*.

I found other flowers, too. Here is a list: blue violets, lungwort, twinflowers, yarrow, goldenrod, asters, pink wintergreen, columbine leaves but no flowers, purple vetch, and wild bergamot. I thought of Rose when I saw the bergamot because she had said she wouldn't like that for a name. I also found starflower, grass-of-Parnassus, meadow-rue and Solomon's seal. Bearberry was also growing all over the forest floor. Paul told us that the aboriginal people called it kinnick-kinnick. I plan to call it by that name from now on because it had that name first.

At the far end of the trail, you come to a campground and the edge of Kingsmere Lake. The wind was fairly strong and there were big waves. I think that this must be what the ocean is like where Shauna is even though she's not my friend. I scouted around, and in behind a bunch of wild roses, I found another plant. I didn't know what it was, so I called Paul and it was *another* orchid. Its name is small round-leaved orchid. He said it was very rare, and he hadn't seen one here before. It is my favorite orchid of all. I don't mind not seeing the extinct white one now that I've seen this one.

It has rose-colored flowers, with white purple-spotted lips, blooming in a spiral along a thick stem. Their pattern reminds me of pretty cloth. I asked if it was okay not to tell the others because they'd already seen the other rare one and this one was so rare, they wouldn't be expecting it, and Paul said yes, that was okay. It could be our little secret. He brought out his camera and took three pictures. I think two of the pictures might have been of me, but I wasn't looking at him when he took them, so I don't know for sure.

When I got back, I had lunch and then I went to work and then I came back to the restaurant for supper. Mom wasn't in the dining room, and when I went upstairs, I found her in my room. I wasn't expecting that—she hardly ever comes in here. Not only was she here, but she had moved her suitcases in here as well.

"I'm staying in with you tonight, okay?" she asked. She was gulping a bit like she does when she's been crying, and I saw that parts of her face were wet.

"Do you want to change your clothes?" I asked. "Or write something in a journal?" She shook her head. "How about if I get you some food? I know you like food," I went on. She shook her head again, and then she laughed a little. I'm not sure what she was laughing at, but I'm glad I cheered her up.

It's going to be a bit of a tight squeeze with both of us in the bed, but I think it will be okay. As long as I can sleep on the side with my clock.

Thursday July 25
A Walk in the Woods with My Mother, Who's Not So Bad After All

Today, Mom had some time off, and she said I
had to spend some time with her, so I said I
wanted to take her for a walk on the Bog Trail.
She tried to convince me to go shopping, but in
the end she agreed to the walk. I ran into the
nature center to let them know that I wouldn't
be available for the Labrador tea making
session, and Julie said that's okay, I could join them
when I got back. By that time the tea might be
ready to drink. Rose said, "No way. You're not getting
any of us to drink that stuff. I've just saved enough money to buy
my own camera, and I want to live to use it!"

We parked our car in the little parking lot at the mouth of
the Bog Trail and headed off into the woods. There were red
squirrels and a chipmunk that stood on its hind legs to watch us
go past. I kept thinking about my narrow escape from shopping
and wanted to tell Mom that the chipmunk's behavior is called
bipedalism and that my gerbils used to stand like this frequently,
but I know she doesn't like hearing about gerbils so I kept quiet.
Gerbils have large eyes, but they rely mainly on their hearing; the

bony capsules of their middle ear are bigger than those of other rodents. Of all my gerbils, June heard particularly well. If I rolled over in bed, she would stand up and have a look to see if I was coming with food. I wonder if Paul's June has extra good hearing.

The woods smelled strongly of rotting logs and damp soil. When trees fall, the wood is eventually broken down and turned back into soil, like in a giant composting bin. I don't admire the smell, but it's not too bad, and then you're on the boardwalk over the wet ground (I do not want to call it a marsh because of you-know-who) and there are different smells pressed together. Mint, mostly, and the tangy sap of the tamaracks. They look like scraggly old men, bent over, with bits of hair and beard hanging down.

My mom didn't want to spend much time poking around in the bog looking for flowers, but I showed her the sundew and she was surprised that we had carnivorous plants on the prairie. Blue damselflies darted about, and the breeze felt confusing because it was hot from the sun and cold from blowing across the water. At the far end of the boardwalk is a bench, and we sat down and I changed my gum. Mom had a drink of juice she'd brought. I just drank water.

"So how are you enjoying your job?" she asked.

I couldn't concentrate very well because the sound of the waves was very distracting, so I just nodded.

"They are good to have you," she said. "This will be a nice thing to put on your résumé, no matter how long you stay."

"They're lucky to have me," I said. "And I will be staying until the end of August."

She didn't say anything much after that, and soon we got up and finished the boardwalk and ended up back in the woods for the return journey. There's a lookout tower built about halfway back, and Mom climbed up to see the top of the forest. I didn't climb it because I don't like heights, and anyway, the inside of the forest is much more interesting than the top.

While Mom was climbing, I found three very unique things to show her. One was a pink polka-dotted mushroom. The other was a little hole in a tree—probably a squirrel's house. The third was a cluster of Indian pipe plants.

The Indian pipe is an unusual flower. One to a stem, there are waxy whitish buds which grow upward and then bend over, pointing down. That's how they got their Latin name, which is *Monotropa*, which means "one direction," and *uniflora*, which means, "one flowered." The group of flowers I found had a grayish blue hue to their petals.

"Watch," I said and touched one of the flowers. It began to turn black, and it wasn't long before the whole thing had gone black.

"Oh, that's horrible," said Mom.

"It's just very sensitive," I said. "It reminds me that there are times when 846 is neither possible nor necessary."

"Uh-huh," she said, standing up and brushing at her pants.

"The Indian pipe has no green leaves with which to synthesize its own food," I told her. "That means that it can't convert carbon dioxide and water into sugar, like normal plants. People used to think it lived as a saprophyte—feeding on sugars contained in dead organic plant matter in the soil. Then they discovered that it can grow in poor soil because it is a parasite—it gets nutrition from the fungus growing on its roots as well as tree roots that grow nearby."

"Oh," she said.

"Thompson's Indians named it wolf's urine," I went on. "They thought the plant grew wherever a wolf urinated."

"I hope there aren't any wolves in here," Mom said.

"Probably not in the daytime," I said. "Wolves hunt at night. It's more likely that there are deer and squirrels, which don't bite, and bears."

Mom started walking.

"You don't have to worry about bears, though," I said, catching up. "They usually go the other way if you make a lot of noise. We could talk a little louder, if you like."

"You are already talking loud," Mom said and walked faster.

On the drive back to town, Mom said, "When do you get your paycheck?"

"Mrs. Thomson said it would be at the end of the month," I said.

"That's good," said Mom. "It will be nice for you to get at least one paycheck."

"I'm going to get two paychecks," I said. "One this month and one next month. Next month's will be more, though, because I will have worked more days."

"Don't you miss a lot of things about home?" Mom asked.

"Yes. But I have learned that you can miss something and not think about it all the time. Like, I miss my room. I miss my music. But I only think about these things at night when I'm going to bed, not usually in the daytime."

"You were very good to come up here," said Mom. "I hope I haven't been asking too much of you. You know, we could go back early if you like."

"No, I can't go back early," I said. "I have my job."

"Oh," said Mom. "Well, we'll see."

I don't know what she meant by that. When we got back to town, I ran to the nature center and Mom went to have a rest.

"We saved you some tea," said Rose. "I think it's awful."

Julie laughed. "It's not so bad. It tastes kind of soothing."

"Like diluted mouthwash!" Rose said.

I looked at the cup Paul was holding out.

"How did you make it exactly?" I asked.

"We went down to the shore and picked some Labrador tea leaves. They're easy to identify because they're all rolled, thick and leathery. Then we took a heaping teaspoon of the broken leaves and added it to boiling water and then added a little honey. Want to try it?"

"No," I said and took the cup. "It smells funny. Like winter-green."

I looked at the picture of the Labrador tea plant that was in a book lying open on the table. "It looks like the rhododendrons we have back home."

"Good connection," said Paul. "It does indeed."

I closed my eyes and took a sip.

"I hate it," I said. "It's full of a temporary loss of good taste."

Rose and Julie laughed, and Paul smiled.

"Good for you for trying it," he said. "Not everyone on our tour tried it."

"I'm going to pour the rest on the grass," I said and I did. I watched for a minute and was relieved to see that the grass didn't die. Then I ran back to the restaurant to have lunch before work. One thing I did right is that I didn't look at the scar on Julie's arm today, not once.

Friday July 26
My Mother is a Pathological Liar

Now I know what Mom meant yesterday when she said, "We'll see." She meant that she had quit her job as well as broken up with Danny and that next Wednesday, after I get paid, we will be going back to Saskatoon. She told me when we were lying in bed together last night.

"But I can't go back until the end of August!" I said. "I promised!"

"Well, we're not staying here," said Mom. "And that's that."

"We have a contract," I told her. "We have a contract saying that we are going to be here for the summer, and at the end of the summer, we are going back to Saskatoon. The contract does not say that we are going home at the end of July because the end of July is not the end of the summer."

"Sometimes it is, and sometimes it isn't," Mom said, and her voice sounded muffled and strange. "Anyway, you don't have any choice in the matter. We are going home on Wednesday."

How can she do this to me? Don't I have any say about anything? She went to sleep after that, but I didn't. I think I stayed awake all night. Today at work, I was supposed to give what's called "my notice," meaning that I would tell them that I was leaving at the end of the month. But I didn't do it.

I'm not going to do it, and no one can make me.

Saturday July 27
Untitled

The rodent is the most successful of modern mammals, both in terms of numbers of species and quantity of individuals. In Asia and Africa, there are over eighty species of rat-like rodents divided into two categories: jirds and gerbils. In 1935, twenty pairs were captured near the Aniur River in East Mongolia. They took them to Japan, and then four breeding pairs were imported to the USA as lab animals. Because they seldom bit and were very sociable, people soon were taking them as pets.

According to known facts about how long other animals have spent on the geological record, gerbils should live until AD fifty million. I don't know if humans will still be in existence. In fact, I could care less. If all the people in the world, along with the white lady's slipper, became extinct tomorrow, I wouldn't care.

!!&%$%@@@

I didn't give my notice today, either.

Sunday July 20
Clock Guts

I am writing this next part days later, but I'm putting the right dates at the top of each section because I don't want to get confused, and think some of it is happening *now*, when it really happened *then*.

On Sunday I was sitting on the steps of the nature center because it was after two and the place was closed. I had slept in, which isn't like me, but after having not slept the last two nights I guess I was just catching up.

At first I forgot it was Sunday because I didn't go to church so it didn't seem like Sunday. I jumped out of bed and saw that someone had bumped my alarm clock off the chair and now it's broken. I took it to Danny before I left and asked him if he'd fix it, and he said he'd try. I have the feeling that he can't fix it because when people say they'll try, it's just another way of letting me down gently. When I rattled the doorknob of the nature center and it was locked, I had this sinking feeling. Why was it locked when everyone was always here in the morning?

I felt just like Stanley in *The Birthday Party* when he went to play the piano at his second concert and the hall was locked. He knew they'd pulled a fast one and gone off and left him. He thought they wanted him to come crawling to them and beg them to open the door for him so that he could play. He ended up back in that room with Meg.

After I remembered that it was Sunday, a lady came by walking her dog and I asked her the time. Two-thirty, she said, and the dog came up and tried to lick me and I had to push it away. I wiped my hand on the grass, in case it actually did lick me because grass is cleaner than dog saliva, but I don't think it did. Then I remembered that the nature center had a reason for being shut, and I felt relieved.

Then I felt bad again because that feeling that I had when the others weren't there would be the same feeling that they would have when I was gone. Next Thursday they would all come to work—Rose, Julie and Paul—and I wouldn't be there. And they would feel lonely for me. Taking other people's perspectives makes you miserable.

The more I thought about this, the worse I felt until I was crying a little as I sat there on the steps. I wondered if maybe Mom had a new boyfriend that she wasn't telling me about, and what if we weren't actually going back to Saskatoon, but somewhere else so she could work in this new boyfriend's restaurant. Then I started thinking how it wasn't fair that Mom had all these boyfriends, and she didn't ever seem to try very hard to get them or care about any of them, while I had none even though I'd really tried hard to have one. Well, maybe I hadn't tried as hard as I could have. I could have talked more to Kody; I know that now.

And maybe I should have let him kiss me more, but a person shouldn't have to let someone kiss them if they don't like it, just to have a boyfriend. You could catch a lot of things.

Then I started crying harder and I even kicked a little and then I felt myself going into full meltdown mode. I pushed off down the grassy hill toward the lake and rolled around kicking trees for a while—for quite a while, actually. When I stopped, I looked at my hands and saw that I had dirt under my fingernails so I went to the water's edge and washed, but then I had the echo of fish on my skin and my IQ went down to about 40.

I kept hearing Mom's voice in my head, "Why do you behave so badly, Taylor?" She hadn't said this to me in a while, but she used to say it all the time before we knew I had Asperger's Syndrome. She said it so much that even though she doesn't say it anymore, I still hear her saying it. "Why do you behave so badly?" and her voice is loud in my ears.

"I don't know," I said loudly. "I can't help it." But after I took some deep breaths and thought for a while more, I knew that I could help it. All I had to do was not leave this place, and I would be okay. I was eighteen years old. Plenty of people stayed on their own when they were eighteen. Mom could go back and I could stay here and have breakfast in the restaurant and go to the nature center in the morning after my walk on the beach and then I could go back to the restaurant for lunch and then I could go to work and then I could go back to the restaurant for supper and then I could walk around in the evening or maybe go to a play, if there were any more plays, or to a movie, even if I didn't like the movie, and I would be company for myself and then I could go to bed. The next day and the day after that and the day after that, I could do the same thing, except for Sundays, which I would have to schedule another way until the end of August when Mom could come and pick me up. I could pay Danny rent, so I wouldn't be a parasite.

The more I thought about this plan, the more I liked it. I rubbed my hands on my dress to get rid of the thoughts about fish, and then I stood up and went back to the restaurant to find Danny. When I found him, I asked him if I could stay even though Mom was going back to Saskatoon, and he said, "Uhhh. Well. What does your mom say about that?"

And I said, "Nine words. Odd number. She likes the idea." I thought she would like it because it seemed to make sense.

"Well, your mom and I can talk about it," he said.

This is when I knew I would have to tell Mom first, and so I said, "Nine words. Okay," and went to find Mom.

She was in our bedroom doing her nails. This is a bad sign. She always does her nails when she's met a new boyfriend, and I felt sick thinking about that possibility. I told her what I wanted to do, and she laughed.

"Don't be silly. How could you stay here by yourself? No, we started this trip together; we'll finish it together."

"But I don't want to go," I said.

"Don't use your loud voice, Taylor," she said. "We're going next Wednesday night, and that's that." I didn't think I was using my loud voice, but the next thing I said I knew was yelling.

"You should try and think about my perspective for a change!" I told her. "You're just living in your own !!&%$%@@@ head and there's other people around who count, too!"

"Never mind. You'll be fine once we're back."

I was so mad I couldn't think of any other words to say. I ran back downstairs, and on my way out, Danny called to me.

"The clock is broken for good," he said. "Can't fix it."

As soon as he said that, I really fell apart. I couldn't imagine what things would be like without that clock. It's the glue that holds me together, the one reasonable thing that I can always count on. And I knew that without it everything was going to be different. I would not be working here this summer. I would not be getting a job in a bookstore in the fall. I would not be taking a class at university. I whirled back, grabbed my clock from his desk and threw it at the wall as hard as I could. I saw it break apart and then I ran.

I took off running toward the golf course. I ran as fast as I could because that was the only way I could stop myself from being overpowered by the blackness that was welling up inside of me.

It was the blackness of The Future, empty again, coming out of my ears and eyes and slithering around my head.

After the golf course, there is a forest and there aren't any paths in it. My legs were getting scratched by bushes, but I kept on running. By the time I was too tired to run anymore, I was completely mixed up and couldn't remember which way I had come or which way I should be going to get back, and I really didn't know whether I wanted to go back.

I had some gum in my pocket, and I chewed it and tried to think about what I wanted to do. I decided that I didn't want to go back, so I sat down and tried to get my bearings. I took Danny's map out of my pocket, but it didn't help. If there had been a policeman around, I could have asked directions. Policemen are never around when you need them.

When I finally decided which way I should go, the mosquitoes were getting so bad that I started running again, but you can't outrun mosquitoes, and I got some very bad bites. I sat down and tried to make myself small so that I could have a bit of a rest and then my right hand started to sting and I pulled it into my lap and looked at it. There were little white welts on it. I looked at the ground and saw some nettles. Stinging nettles. They sure do live up to their name. Or rather, names. They are also called burning nettle, seven-minute itch, Indian spinach, common nettle and dwarf nettle. I just call them stinging nettles.

After I realized I had been stung, I tried to remember what could cure the welts. I had read that rubbing crushed nettles on the skin would actually cure the irritated area, but you were supposed to use gloves and I didn't have any. I also knew that dock, plantain, jewelweed and fiddlehead ferns were all supposed to provide good treatments, and so I got up and started looking around for one of these. I finally found a few ferns, removed the scruffy coating and rubbed it on my hand. I think it helped a little.

Nettles can be eaten as long as they are boiled well. Some people have tried to eat them raw, but they can give you a stinging lip. I was feeling hungry, but not that hungry. After a few minutes, I found a patch of raspberries and tried one. I didn't like it, but I ate a few more. My lips stung with the raspberries. I might as well have eaten the nettles.

A little later, I found some plantain leaves and rubbed them on my arms and legs. They are supposed to be a natural insect repellent, and they helped. I put some leaves in my pocket for later. I felt hungry again and ate some rose petals, but they weren't very filling.

I saw three deer and four elk, and one of the deer was a fawn and two of the elk had antlers. I figured that since the elk were like deer they wouldn't bite. I also saw a number of different kinds of birds. As time went on, I counted the birds to seven and then started over. I tried not to think about snakes. Inside my head I felt heavy.

It began to get dark, and I dug away at a little hollow filled with kinnick-kinnick and dry leaves until I had a sort of nest for myself. The mosquitoes were humming around my head, but at least they didn't bite, much. I remembered about the oriental sore that gerbils get from being bitten by infected sandflies, and I hoped that the mosquitoes wouldn't give me anything more than just an itchy bite. Some mosquitoes carry West Nile virus, but maybe that kind doesn't live this far north. I thought about bears and then decided that if one came up to me I would yell and scream and make all sorts of noise, and then it would run away.

I dug around in my purse and pulled out all the things in it. I had three more pieces of gum, and I chewed them while I looked at the other things. I had a card in my wallet with Shauna's address in Greece on it. I remember that when she gave it to me, she asked me to write her and said, if I did, she would write a postcard back. I forgot that I was supposed to write first. It is a relief to know that she is still my friend, after all.

I'm thinking of Rose and Julia and Paul. They are my friends, too. Having friends is quite agreeable. Four friends. I have four friends. I'm not counting my teacher, Mrs. Thomson, as a friend because only little kids think of teachers as their friends. She is a good teacher, but I draw the line at that.

After I dug around in my purse, I thought about what I should do tomorrow. I thought about the wild orchid I'd never seen, called the Venus's slipper. *Calypso bulbosa.* It's probably out of season now, and I knew I'd never find it. I cried into the leaves for a while, thinking of my damaged clock and how it will never look like itself again, and then I recalled that the fat-tailed gerbil of North Africa has a tail which is so full of fat that it resembles a small sausage and this thought was mildly comforting. Then I must have slept because before too long it was morning. I was very surprised that I'd slept without my clock. I was sure that without my clock I would never sleep again. But I was wrong.

Monday July 29
Sleeping in the Woods is Not
Running Away

When I woke up, I shook my arms and legs, which were very stiff, and thought about getting to work by 1:00 P.M., and this was a problem because I didn't know which way work was. I relieved myself in the bushes and tried not to think about what I was doing because it was quite disgusting. Then I started walking. I thought I heard the hum of traffic, and I walked toward it. I didn't feel very hungry, but I ate a few more rose petals along the way. The mosquitoes were really biting again, and I took some of the plantain leaves out of my pocket and rubbed them on my skin.

It was hard walking in the woods because I had to keep lifting my feet up over branches and fallen tree trunks. I felt a bit closed in, but I kept reminding myself that this was just like being in church, and there was no ceiling. Eventually, I reached a paved road. I walked along the ditch and ate some wild blueberries and they tasted very mild and I liked them and each time I found some I stopped and ate them.

After what seemed like hours, I saw the golf course up on a hill, and I knew I was going in the right direction. I switched to the other side of the road so that I would see oncoming cars better and then found a trail along the lake. I could smell the water and hear the waves. It felt comforting to smell and hear these familiar things.

When I got to the nature center, I went in and asked Rose what time it was, and she said it was time to tell everybody what I'd been up to because my mom and Danny and Julie and Paul were all freaking out. She picked up the telephone.

"Did you run away?" she asked as she dialed the number.

"I didn't run for very long," I said. "I mostly walked."

Paul was in the film booth, and he came running out to me and said, "I'm so glad to see you. I was worried about you," and I started to cry and there were some strangers in the nature center using the computer programs about animals and plants and I kept looking over at them to see if they were staring at my crying. Paul led me out of the center and sat me down on a bench.

"Are you okay?" he asked.

"Am I late for work?" I asked.

"Don't worry about work," he said. "It's not important."

"It is important! My mom doesn't think so, but I do. She wants me to go back to Saskatoon on Wednesday night and quit my job, but I can't do that because then things won't be the same. And I said I'd work until the end of August and I should keep my word because this is my first job and I'll never get another one." The words kept tumbling out and Paul put his arm around me and it felt nice and then he touched my cheek where I had some bites and he asked me if they hurt and I said no. And then he kissed me and that was nice, too. It was very different from when Kody kissed me. I didn't think about germs at all.

Then I heard my mother yelling.

"You bastard! You get away from her!"

Paul is Not a Criminal

At first I thought she had said, "Taylor, why are you behaving so badly?" because she was using that kind of voice. She said the same thing again, and I realized she was saying, "You bastard, you get away from her," and she was saying it to Paul.

He jumped away from me and took his arm from around my shoulders.

"You pervert. You child molester!" she screamed.

"Just wait a minute!" he said. "Just wait a freakin' minute here. You've got the wrong idea!"

"Don't you talk to me!" she said. "You just get away from my daughter because I am calling the police!"

I decided I had to say something to stop her, so I stood up and yelled, "You are behaving very badly." That did stop her and she looked at me with her mouth open.

"I have work to do," I said. "And I am going inside to do my shift."

"You stop right there, young lady," she said. "You will stop and tell me everything that's gone on and where you spent the night and then we're going to tell the same story to the police."

"Why would I talk to the police?" I asked. "I haven't stolen anything. And I'm not lost anymore."

My mother paused. It was a long pause.

"Because we have been looking for you all night," she said finally.

"I would have been back sooner, but the map wasn't very good," I said.

"You were lost?" she said very slowly.

"Well, first I was running and I couldn't decide whether to run away or run home. Then when I decided to run home, I was too tired to run anymore and I couldn't remember which way home was. I walked and walked, and eventually slept in some leaves."

"You poor thing," said Mom. "Look at your face. Look at all the bites on your arms!"

"And then this morning I heard traffic sounds and I walked toward them and found the road and walked along it and got here just in time."

"You must be starving. Come on back with me and I'll get you something. Then we'll just drive home today."

I looked at Paul. He was fiddling around with the cigarettes in his pocket.

"It is both possible and necessary that I stay here!" I said. "It's not fair that we have to go home. This is my first job and I'm eighteen and a half years old and I think it's about time I had a job! It's not fair that I have to quit or leave my friends, either! I do have friends here, you know!"

"I can see that," said Mom, looking at Paul. I knew she was still mad at him.

Paul was still looking at me.

"I'm sorry," he said softly. "I was out of line. I shouldn't have kissed you."

"It was okay," I said.

"It wasn't okay. I was just so glad you were all right."

All three of us stood there, looking at each other, but mostly Mom and Paul looked at me. I don't like being looked at very much.

"This is a Pinter pause," I said, which made Mom raise her eyebrows and Paul smile.

"Could I go and get a quick lunch, and then come back and take over from Rose?" I asked Paul.

"You should take the day off," he said. "It's okay to do that once in a while."

"Really?" I asked. "Mrs. Thomson wouldn't mind?"

"You could phone her."

"My English teacher Mrs. Thomson would never let anyone take the day off," I said. "Plus, who will run the shop?"

"I can take the afternoon shift today," said Rose, from the doorway. "I have nothing else to do."

So I made the phone call, and then I went to my room and lay down. It felt weird to be lying on my bed without my clock, but I managed.

When I woke up my mother brought me some lunch, and after I had finished, she sat on the end of my bed and said, "Taylor, I want to know all about Paul."

"What do you want to know?" I asked.

"Well, for starters, has he ever tried to kiss you before?"

"No," I said.

"Do you ever go off by yourself with him? What does he say to you?"

This is the kind of conversation I find really hard—when there are two or more questions and you're supposed to answer one while keeping your mind on the other one.

"Well, we biked to the outdoor theater. I told you about it; that's where I found the yellow lady's slipper. Did you know that it has been used in tinctures to cure insomnia and anxiety?"

"I'm not interested in the !!&%$%@@@ lady's slipper!" Mom yelled. "Just answer the questions!" I thought about telling her that she was talking in the red zone, but I didn't. It was startling to hear mom swear. I didn't mention it.

"So tell me about the times you were alone with him!"

"Well, once we went on that trail by the lake where we saw the bears. After I jumped in the lake, he bought me an ice cream cone."

"Did he want to do anything with you after the ice cream cone?"

"What do you mean?"

"Like did he want to kiss you or touch you or anything?"

"No. I came back here and had french fries, but I wasn't that hungry, so I didn't eat many."

There was a silence.

"You were wearing the short green skirt with the white blouse," I said, trying to be helpful. "Remember?"

"I don't care what I was wearing," she said. "I just care about what this Paul character has done to you." I could see the big H in her forehead and I knew what that meant.

"He isn't a character. He isn't in a play. He's real and he's my friend," I said. "I have four friends. Paul, Julia, Rose and Shauna. Today, I'm going to write to Shauna because I have her address."

"First I need to hear more about Paul. What kinds of things does he say to you? Did you ever go alone with him into the woods at any other time?"

I figured out that Mom still thought Paul was a bastard, and she was trying to collect evidence, like maybe that he had tried to have sex with me or something. I know all about having sex, although I haven't had it with anyone. And I know better than to have it with someone in the woods, which is what Mom was trying to suggest. That would be as bad as having sex in church.

"We talk about all sorts of things," I said, the words rattling out faster and faster. "Like gerbils—" I knew she wouldn't like this because she doesn't like me talking about gerbils, so I quickly added, "and people committing suicide and he asked me about my boyfriend and we talked about his relationship with his wife. And how he doesn't think I look threatening and he talked about my shirt and what is possible and necessary."

"I knew it!" she said loudly. "I knew he was telling you inappropriate things!"

"What inappropriate things?" I yelled back. "Paul is not inappropriate, and you shouldn't say bad stuff about him!"

"You are not to see that Paul person again, and what's more, I'm going to get the police to put a restraining order on him!"

I didn't know what a restraining order was, but I figured it was something bad, so I yelled, "I don't have to listen to this. You don't know anything about what's possible or necessary and just because you're my mother you think you can be the boss of me and you aren't. I'm the boss of myself. And I'm not going back to Saskatoon and I'm eighteen and a half and you can't make me and even if you do make me I'll just run away again and keep running until I'm so far away from you that . . . that—" I stopped. I couldn't think of anything more to say.

Mom had been pacing back and forth, but now she sat down on a chair and began to cry. I watched her for a while, and then she stopped and I handed her a box of tissues.

"You're right," she said, hiccupping a little. "I'm not the boss of you. But I care very much about you, and I'm trying to make good decisions for both of us."

"I know you care about me," I said. "You were the one who stayed and Dad left because of me."

"You know that he didn't leave because of you," Mom said. "We've talked about this. I let him go, but you don't have to. He'll always be your dad."

I took a deep breath. I thought of saying that gerbil males were allowed to stay in the breeding nest, but I swallowed the words.

"I will only listen to you if you forget about the restraining order," I went on. "Paul hasn't done anything wrong. He's just been my friend. He hasn't touched me or hurt me in any way, and all he's done is listen to me when I talk and sometimes talk back. Talk back in a good way, I mean."

"Really?" asked Mom. She still had the H in her forehead.

"Really," I said.

"Because if anyone ever did anything you didn't want them to do or anything that bothered you, I want you to tell me about it."

"I will," I said.

"Good," said Mom.

"Okay, now," I said, holding onto my IQ as hard as I could. "Why can't we stay here?"

"Because I have to start my other job on Thursday. If I'm not working here, I have to work somewhere," said Mom.

"I thought you gave it up for the summer," I said.

"I did. But that was when I knew I'd be working here. We need a paycheck coming in, Taylor. That's all there is to it."

"I have a paycheck coming in," I said. "Please don't underestimate me."

"It's not enough. We have rent to pay and bills for the telephone and the power. And food. And then I buy clothes that you don't wear."

We sat together quietly for a while. Then I said, "I didn't know that part about the money."

"I'm sorry. I did underestimate you. I should have told you all about it. I just thought it was simpler if you didn't have to worry. And I really thought you wouldn't mind going back to Saskatoon. I thought you were just making a fuss because it was a change again, but that you really, deep down, wanted to go. I know you miss your room."

"I do miss my room. And it wouldn't be bad to go back. I could buy another alarm clock, but I don't really want one. I would like an atomic watch because it gets its time from a satellite beaming through Boulder, Colorado, and it is always correct. But what about my job? There will be an empty space where I'm supposed to be."

"They'll find someone else. Don't worry. Didn't they tell you that when you gave your notice?" I opened the drawer beside my bed and took out a package of gum. I offered some to her and then had a piece myself.

"I didn't give my notice. It didn't seem appropriate," I said finally.

Mom burst out laughing.

"You are going to drive me insane," she said when she'd stopped. "But I suppose that makes us even." She picked up my hands and started rubbing them the way I like.

"I'm not insane," I said. "I have Asperger's Syndrome, which is not a mental illness."

"I know. I was just trying to make a joke," Mom said, so I smiled even though I didn't get the joke, not really.

"It used to be considered a mental illness," I said. "Kanner, who first published articles on autism in 1943, classified it as a subset of childhood schizophrenia. One year later, Hans Asperger published a study of people who were autistic and described them in a category unto themselves. The term, Asperger's Syndrome, was coined in 1981, after his death, to indicate a particular form of autism."

"I know all this," said Mom softly. "We learned this together."

"Oops, I forgot," I said. "I can't remember what you know and what I know and keep them separate. Forgetting's only relative, anyway," I went on, "to what you have to remember. Lots of things you don't really need to know, and then it doesn't matter if they disappear. And then there are things that you remember, but you wish they'd disappear. Like, the way what's his name's fingers are always oily and leaving prints on things. I sure won't miss him."

Mom sighed.

"I guess I won't miss him, either. Maybe he wasn't a nine, like I said."

"Maybe he was more like a three," I said.

"A three dressed up as a nine," Mom said and laughed so hard she had tears rolling down her face. I don't know why she thought it was funny, but I smiled, too, because that's polite. It's incorrect to identify people as numbers in the first place. Numbers are only relative to each other. The reason numbers are meaningful is because they are more or less than other numbers. If you start associating them with people, it just messes things up.

"I guess there's other fish in the sea," she said. "I just wonder why I can't seem to keep a relationship going. I want someone to love me and why is that so hard to manage?"

"I love you," I said. "If you want me to go and get you some food, I will. Maybe some apples. You like apples."

"No thanks," said Mom, and she folded my hands in hers. "I wish relationships weren't so complicated."

"You're telling me," I said. "I am still looking for a boyfriend. At least you've had some. An unusually high number of them." Mom put my hands down.

"Do you understand that we have to go back?" she said.

"I guess so." I took a deep breath. "I might be able to handle it."

"I know you can," she said and squeezed my arm. "I'll go over to the nature center and let them know. You just rest here."

"Wait," I said. "No, I'll go. I'm the one who's letting them down. I should tell them about it."

"Taylor," Mom started, but I interrupted her. I don't usually interrupt people because I know it's bad manners, but I just had to this time.

"I got this job by myself, and I will take care of quitting," I said. "Remember, you're not the boss of me."

"You're right," said Mom. "I'll wait here and you can come back and tell me all about it."

I couldn't believe my victory.

"But if you're any longer than half an hour, I'm calling the police," she said.

I looked at her.

"Just kidding," she said. I don't know how she could kid at a time like this.

Quitting My Job

So I went over to the nature center, and it was five o'clock. Rose was closing the till and counting money into plastic bags, just like I had done on other days. Julia was dusting the displays and Paul was sweeping the floor.

"Hello," I said. "I just came back to say that Wednesday will be my last day working here. I'm really sorry." I felt tears come into my eyes, but I blinked them back. "I've really liked working here, and I'm glad that you are all my friends."

The door at the back opened and a group of people came out. They must have been watching a film. I let them file out of the building before I finished what I had to say. Rose, Julie and Paul came to stand near me.

"My mom has to go back to her old job," I said. "We need the money, and so I have agreed to go back to Saskatoon with her. I feel really awful about leaving you with an empty space, and I'm sorry I didn't tell you sooner. I hope you can find someone else in time, and I hope the new person will be as good as me even though she won't be me."

"It'll be okay," Paul said. "I'm sure Nell Thomson can find somebody. The most important thing is that you're okay with going back. Are you? Did you talk to your mother about it?"

"Yes," I said. "It seems reasonable, now that she's explained things."

"Well, at least you have three more days," said Rose. "That's enough time to plan a good-bye party, anyway."

"Is a good-bye party like a birthday party?" I asked. "Because if it is, I'm not interested."

"I was thinking about going for ice cream," said Rose. "Maybe Wednesday after work."

"If a good-bye party is going for ice-cream," I said, "you can count me in. As long as there's vanilla."

I smiled.

"That's a joke," I said. "Of course there'd be vanilla. It's the most commonest kind!"

"Would you like me to write you a letter of reference?" asked Julie. "I'd be very happy to. I'd put down how you remember all the names of the plants and how you helped me as a volunteer on my trail walks."

"Thank you," I said. "I suppose I'll need a letter like that when I go to see about a job in Saskatoon. I don't really like envelopes. Could you please not put it into an envelope?"

"Okay," said Julie. "And you know, you really should ask Nell Thomson for one as well."

"I will," I said.

Paul walked with me outside and we sat down on a bench.

"I need to talk to you," he said. "About what happened this morning."

"What happened?" I said.

"When I said I shouldn't have kissed you."

"It's because I have special needs, isn't it?" I said.

"No, that's not it at all," Paul said. "I didn't think about what I was doing. I guess I was out of line."

"It's okay," I said. "I'm not mad and I didn't worry about germs at all."

"Because I'm married. And that's an important . . . uh—"

"Obligation," I said.

"What?"

"Being married is a legal obligation," I said. "It's okay. You did not behave badly even though my mom wanted to put you in jail. You are my friend."

"I'm glad," said Paul. "Someday someone else will want to kiss you, and it will be the right thing to do."

"Maybe," I said. "As long as it isn't Kody."

"I'm sure it won't be," he said. Then he took my hand.

"It's been really nice knowing you," he said. "I hope we'll see each other again sometime."

"We will," I said. "I'll see you for the next three days."

Then he laughed, but that's okay because I laughed, too.

When I got back to the restaurant, I phoned Mrs. Thomson. She wasn't mad at all. She said thanks for letting her know and promised to write me the reference letter. She said it's too bad it's been so calm lately, or she'd have offered me a spin on her boat. I said that's okay. I had a spin on someone else's boat.

Tuesday July 30
Fishing for Men

I didn't sleep very well again last night because Mom was too hot lying next to me and she made me hot. She could be going through menopause. Maybe she needs an ice pack or medication. It will be great being at home in my own room in my own bed without Mom in it.

This morning the interpretive program at the nature center was all about fish. At first, I didn't want to go, but then I thought I should take a chance. I know that fish cannot hurt me. Unless they are sharks and there are no sharks here. We met at the front door and looked at a brochure about common fish that live in Waskesiu Lake. I asked why the programs were called interpretive programs, and Julie said it's because they help people understand the park better and translate the language of nature. So it's not just me that needs a translator once in a while.

We drove to Birch Bay in four vehicles, and about ten people watched as Paul and Julie waded out into the lake and put a net into the water. Then they came back and talked about the types of fish that live in the lake and how laws keep fishing controlled so that the numbers of fish don't drop too low. After half an hour, they waded out again and pulled in the net.

It was full of fish! They looked horrible. I got the shivers thinking about how I had been swimming in the lake with them, but then I had a good thought. I had survived.

There were three jackfish—two large ones and one small one. There was a pickerel and something called a sauger, which is a cross between a jack and a pickerel. Then there was a small perch and two sucker fish, which are the ugliest fish I have ever seen, with long lips that hang down and suck slime off rocks and things in the lake. Paul and Julie carefully untangled the fish from the net, held each one up for a minute (they were wearing gloves) and then let it go. I liked watching the fish dart away after they were released. They looked glad to be free.

Maybe this is kind of like how Mom lets her boyfriends go. First she goes about fishing around until she catches one. She keeps him and examines him for a while and then pushes him out into the water again where he can swim away. Someday, she might catch a fish she will want to keep. I hope it won't be a sucker.

This afternoon, I had my most maximum sales ever. It rained for ninety-four minutes, and we had thirty-two people come into the nature center. I think they wished they were at the beach because most of them were wearing bathing suits with just T-shirts over top. I sold six books, fifteen postcards and five children's puzzle cubes. No boys my age came in.

Wednesday July 31
My Future Plans

Mrs. Thomson came into the nature center this
morning and gave me my check. Then she went
windsurfing. It must be nice to own a bookstore and have people working in it so you can
go windsurfing while they make money for
you, even though I wouldn't like windsurfing.
She also left me the reference letter about
what a good worker I was, to add to Julie's. That's
two letters of reference I'll have to take to the bookstore in Saskatoon. She said she was going to phone
her friend there, too, and put in a good word for me. Mom said
that this was going beyond the call of duty. I'm not sure what
that means.

Danny had breakfast with Mom and me in the restaurant,
even though he had taken her name *Penny* off the sign. Now it
just says *Pizza Pen,* which I think really sucks. He said that we
should celebrate with champagne and orange juice, and even
though he and Mom were breaking up, they could at least be civil
to each other. Mom said yes, but I knew she didn't really want to
be civil. She took a lot of small bites and used her knife a lot. I

started counting the bites she was taking until she told me to stop. Her voice was like a fishhook without any bait on it. I didn't like it. I also didn't like my drink. It tasted like tuna.

I asked the waitress if they had any blueberries, and she said they did not. Mom looked surprised and asked if I liked blueberries. I said I did.

"Will wonders never cease?" she said. Then she offered to buy some when we were back in Saskatoon.

"And I would like to buy an atomic watch," I said. "First the atomic watch, then the blueberries."

I ate most of my pancakes. Mom had an omelet. Danny had sausages, eggs over easy, toast and oatmeal porridge. His mouth when he was chewing looked like a dog's bottom.

"I never did see a Venus's slipper," I said. "That is a real disappointment. I'll have to come back in the spring so I can search for it again."

Mom had that H on her forehead, but she didn't say anything.

"Was it any trouble getting your old job back?" Danny asked her. Mom shook her head. *Nine words,* I thought.

"And you, Taylor," said Danny. "What are your plans for fall?"

"Nine again," I said. Mom opened her mouth in a mad way, but before she could say anything I answered the question. "I will try to get a job in a bookstore," I said. "I have two letters of reference, and they both declare that I am well suited to working in bookstores. After I get a job in a bookstore, I will register for one class at the university. A biology class. And if I have Thanksgiving off, I will go and visit Dad because he asked me. And I will take my new atomic watch."

"Are you sure you don't want to do a cooking course, first?" asked Mom. "Cooking courses always come in handy. Restaurants often need help in the kitchen."

"I'm not very enthusiastic in the kitchen," I said. "But I am good with plants and animals. All my friends say so."

I looked at Danny. He was not my friend. If I passed him on the street, I probably wouldn't even recognize him. My friends are Rose, Julia, Paul and Shauna. Four friends. Four friends are better than none.

More things happened today, but I can't write about them now. I am home and it feels too weird. I need more gum. I will write more later.

Friday August 2
My Wish for a Boyfriend Came True

I am sitting in my own blue room listening to my classical baroque. It is a relief to be home. I have an atomic watch on my wrist that I bought with my own money. You'd never know by looking that it tells time by reading the vibrations of atoms. My mother is in the bathtub, singing. This is her third bath since we got back. I have noticed that she bathes a lot when she gets rid of a boyfriend. I think she is glad to be home, too.

I have more to write about Wednesday. Wednesday morning, after breakfast, Paul and I took the bikes and went for one last ride. Then we came back and I had lunch with Mom. Then I went to work as usual, for the last time. Just as my shift was starting, a woman came in with a big puzzle that she wanted to return because it was missing a piece, and I had to learn how to record a return. Good thing Rose was still around to show me. Knowing how to return an item will be important when I work in the city because probably a lot more people return things in city bookstores.

Paul asked me what I planned to do with the money I had made. I said I'd be putting it toward my university class. And maybe buying another gerbil.

Rose came back and Paul, Julie, Rose and I went for ice cream. I had vanilla. Julie had diet strawberry. Rose had black licorice, and Paul had rum 'n' raisin again. I tried not to look at it. Then Paul took out two pictures. He said that I could keep them.

"What are they?" I asked.

"I took them, remember, on the Kingsmere Trail? When you found the small round-leaved orchid."

I looked at the pictures. I remembered that Paul had taken them that day in the woods. I looked closely at the orchid. It was beautiful. I looked at the other picture.

Chin. Clothing. Hair. It was a person. It was me. I like looking at this picture. I like thinking of how it feels to be in the forest. I can remember the minty smell of the woods, the cathedral ceiling. In the picture, it looks like there might be snakes there, but I know there aren't.

I got back just in time to help Mom load up my suitcase, and my friends stood on the curb and waved as we drove off.

"Good-bye," I called.

"They can't hear you, Taylor. You have the windows up," Mom said.

I rolled down the windows and called, "Good-bye!" and I heard them call back to me, like an echo.

We drove out of town, and Mom put on the radio and smiled at me.

"Good-bye Waskesiu; hello Saskatoon," she said.

I squeezed shut my eyes and tried to remember what my room looked like. My blue room. It seemed so long ago that I was in it.

I thought about my dad leaving in the Volvo and not coming back. I thought about how hard it had been for me to move to Waskesiu and how I'd been brave and how I'd conquered The Future, for now, anyway. I thought about how I'd hoped to have a boyfriend and how I had thought Kody was one, but he really hadn't been, and how in fact no one had been. Then I decided that while he was kissing me, Paul had been my boyfriend, even if it only lasted a few seconds. I smiled to myself. My first boyfriend. I have crossed over the line. And once you cross over, it's permanent.

If I count my friends on my fingers—Rose, Julie, Paul and Shauna—it makes four. Mom makes five, and even though sometimes she's a pathological liar, she can also be a friend. I'll also count my dad. He is sort of borderline, but it's possible that Thanksgiving will work out. That makes six. Six friends. One day soon, I'm going to get a new gerbil. That will make seven. And seven is a lucky number.